CW00833741

A Christmas Malice

A Christmas Malice was first published in Great Britain in 2014 by Gaslight Crime. Copyright © Anne and John Bainbridge 2014/2019. Cover image © Paul Bowden/Shutterstock 2014. The right of John Bainbridge to be identified as the author of this work has been asserted by him in accordance with the Copyright, Designs and Patent Act 1988. **All rights reserved.** No part of this publication may be reproduced, stored in or introduced into a retrieval system, or transmitted, in any form, or by any means (electronic, mechanical, photocopying, recording or otherwise) without the prior written permission of the author. Any person who does any unauthorised act in relation to this publication may be liable to criminal prosecution and civil claims for damages. This publication must not be circulated in any form of binding or cover other than that in which it is now published and without a similar condition including this condition being imposed on the subsequent purchaser.

All characters and places in this novel are fictitious and the creation of the author's imagination, and any resemblance to places or real persons, living or dead, firms and institutions, is purely coincidental.

www.johnbainbridgewriter.wordpress.com

Our Books

A Seaside Mourning
The Seafront Corpse
The Holly House Mystery
Balmoral Kill
Dangerous Game
The Shadow of William Quest
Deadly Quest
Dark Shadow
Loxley
Wolfshead
Villain
Legend

One

December 1873

It took a surprising effort to dress the clothes on the body.

Taking them had been the easy part. No one locked their doors in daylight in the village. Moving like a wraith through the rear yard of the shop premises, turning the handle of the scullery door and inside in an instant.

It was the home of a man who lived alone. A lingering smell of bacon fried in lard, the skillet on the draining-board, a smear of grease along its rim. The rug in front of the range was rucked. The weekly *Lynn Advertiser* on the battered table, folded and propped against the teapot.

Listening at the bottom of the stairs, the door through to the shop was left ajar, the blinds half-down, making the interior shadowed. Shelves of brown, blue and green glass bottles, a wooden mould for pressing pills. The brass scales behind the counter, a large pestle and mortar between two carboys in the window.

Viewing it all from this angle was like being behind a stage, peeping through a gap in the curtains. The quality of silence confirmed no one else was there, though who could be? The more you listened, the more you became aware of tiny sounds, not really silence at all. The tap dripping, then a click as the hand moved on the mantel clock. And once, a faint scuffle behind a skirting-board.

The stairs creaked, so did the wardrobe door, with its escaping odour of mothballs. It was satisfying to thrust his best jacket and new hat into a sack. Then retreat carefully through the cold house, wherein everything was hasty and careless.

Sneak along the path behind the houses, encumbered. But it was too late in the day for women to be beating rugs or shaking dusters from their windows.

Then disappear through the trees to the abandoned shack by the edge of a turnip field. Within living memory it had been the home of an old man. They said he'd been a tinkler who'd settled in the parish. Villagers thereabouts had taken their pans to him, until his fingers had become too misshapen to mend them.

One winter, the wisps of smoke from the pipe that served as chimney, had been seen no more. It was said his corpse had been found frozen on the earthen floor.

The jacket already looked the worse for wear, smudged with flour from inside the sack. It was awkward work pushing and pulling the rigid arms into the sleeves. Fastening the horn buttons with cold, clumsy fingers. The sniff of frost was in the air.

Winter came early to Norfolk and it was imminent. The rich colours of autumn had left the trees, bled into dried husks crumpled underfoot. The birches and ash huddled together, braced for the snow that always came from across the German ocean.

The final touch would be his billycock, tilted at a jaunty angle. A bowler they called it elsewhere. There was no going back now and it served him right. No one about in the last hour of daylight. There was no work needed to bring the farm labourers to this part.

They'd been ditching on the Fen side of the village that morning. Old Bart Swaley and young John Christopher would have downed tools and be making for the Barley Mow by this time. Here, there was no one to see the bitter thing done. Only the black crows picking along the dark furrows.

~

Bishopsgate terminus had been crowded and noisy, with steam belching, whistles blowing and doors slamming on the dark blue coaches of the Great Eastern Railway. This would certainly be the last time he journeyed from there, as the Liverpool Street station was almost finished and due to open early in the new year.

It was a relief to climb into the carriage in readiness to leave the capital. The train, however, was packed with passengers in second and third. He found himself crammed between a window seat and a stout lady, a carpet bag clutched on her lap. A conversation ensuing between the other occupants confirmed, they too, were journeying to stay with relatives for Christmas.

By the time the light dulled across the flat land, on the shortest day of the year, Inspector Josiah Abbs felt an unaccustomed, nervous anticipation as the train approached his destination. It was eighteen months or more since he had seen Hetty. Their first meeting since she had been widowed.

As the locomotive began to slow, he rose to his feet and grasped his travelling case. This was his first visit to the village where his sister and her husband had moved. He looked out with interest, as the swaying motion steadied and finally stilled. Thirty miles or more from their childhood home, Aylmer was situated on the edge of an unknown Norfolk, the county being large and composed of varied topography.

They had been raised in an area parcelled between rich landowners, with prosperous farms, neat estate villages and shooting coverts. Hereabouts, the land skirted the Fens to south and west. Wide, lonely vistas of dark, fertile land, with scarcely a hedgerow or tree. The land was carved by water, dykes, drains and the sullen Great Ouse flowing to the ancient port of King's Lynn.

He was the only passenger alighting on the short platform. The train did not linger. The small country station was scarcely more than a halt. Its modest, single storey building, with Dutch gables, hardly looked large enough to contain living accommodation. Then, all first impressions were pushed aside as his sister appeared in the open doorway.

The diffidence he felt at meeting after a long absence was quickly dispelled by her familiar smile. Abbs felt himself transported back to the school gate. Where his sister would on occasion wait, with an uncanny foreknowledge of the days he intended to slip away to woods and river bank. Rather than coming straight home to attend to his tasks.

He was now taller than her, he reflected as he bent to kiss her cheek. And they were two siblings, instead of five.

'There now, Dora said I'd be late but I made it with five minutes to spare. She's looking forward to meeting you. We'll soon be home, Arthur insisted I take the trap.'

She spoke over her shoulder as she led the way through the booking office, where a bright fire was spitting in a tiny grate.

The stationmaster gave him an appraising look as he inspected his ticket. 'This'll be your brother then, Mrs Byers? Happen we could do with another policeman. We don't get many strangers in Aylmer,' he announced to Abbs, pronouncing it Elmer. 'Good night to you, sir.'

Abbs took his seat in the smartly painted conveyance, with *Chas. Byers, Grocer and Provisions Dealer* in brown lettering along the side.

'What did he mean, Hetty?'

His sister was silent, as she untethered the reins and climbed up beside him to move off. She didn't answer until she'd turned the grey horse and they were out of the station yard, passing a small chapel.

'It's nothing, really. There've been one or two odd happenings lately around the village. Not crimes,' she said, hastily, turning to look at him. 'Only mischief, nothing to concern you at all. I don't know why Thomas said that.'

'You do have a village constable here?'

'Yes, Constable Duffield. He's a good policeman but he's as baffled as the rest of us. You know, you're looking tired and too thin. I don't suppose you feed yourself properly.'

Abbs was amused, reminded of their mother's scolding. 'Well enough, I generally get something on the way home.'

'That's not the same as wholesome cooking. You never did have much appetite as a boy. I dare say you live on bread and cheese indoors. I shall feed you up while you're here and we'll talk properly. I shall want to hear all your news.'

It was easier to speak moving along in the dusk, than it would be seated indoors, especially with someone else in the house.

'Hetty, about Charley's funeral, I'm truly sorry I was unable to visit you in those last months.'

'There's no need, Josiah. A man in your position can't be spared, I knew that and he went downhill quickly. Arthur was here and there was nothing anyone could have done.'

'I'm glad of your letters, even though I don't reply as often as I should.'

'No matter, it's easier for a woman to find time to write. I think you'll like Dora, Miss Stephens. The year's gone swiftly,

4

she's been boarding with me since spring. I do enjoy her companionship and it saves me rattling round an empty house.'

'I'm thankful she came to you. You've plenty of work, then?'

'Yes, indeed, enough and more for the pair of us.'

'You would say if you needed any help?'

'Bless you, Josiah, I do very well and Arthur keeps me supplied from the shop. He's a good man, a mite overwhelming at times,' Hetty smiled mischievously at him, 'but he has a kind heart.'

She held the reins lightly and the horse trotted steadily along the lane, with fields at either hand. The first evening star had appeared, hanging cold and distant above them.

'It'll freeze tonight, it's so clear.'

Looking at the sky, Abbs reminded himself how wide the heavens appeared in Norfolk. Like a dark blanket tucked in over the landscape, making you feel small and insignificant.

'I see the station's apart from the village.'

'We're coming up to it now. By the way, Josiah, best not to mention those odd things to Dora. She had an unpleasant trick played on her. It shook us both up.' Hetty looked ahead again, clearly not intending to say more.

'You can't leave it at that,' said Abbs lightly. 'I'm bound to ask what?'

'She had a parcel.' Hetty continued with some reluctance. 'In a pretty box, the sort that contains an article of female attire. Dora was excited, she naturally thought it was a present. When she opened it, inside swathes of paper, she found a pig's head.' She shook her head at the memory. 'We've all seen them. It was the unexpectedness of it that was so nasty.'

She slowed to turn into a bend and Abbs caught sight of the first lit window. 'I suppose it was children's idea of a joke.'

Frowning, Abbs considered. 'Was it sent through the post?'

'Left in the porch.'

'I won't say anything.'

Privately, he thought it unlikely that village children had dreamt up such a notion or had the means to hand. He wanted to ask if Miss Stephens had done something to make an enemy, but he sensed further questions would be unwelcome. Even so, this had upset his sister and he resolved to learn more if he could.

'Here we are. This is the house and that was Charley's shop next door.'

After passing a lamp indicating the police house and an inn called The White Lion, they'd turned into a side street, just off the main thoroughfare of cottages and shops. They drew up outside a double-fronted shop, that still had his brother-in-law's name over the door.

Abbs just had time to take in the terraced house and the dark premises on the right, before the buff-aproned figure of Hetty's step-son appeared.

'You found your way to us at last, then. That's capital.' Arthur Byers beamed up at him, as he took the bridle in one hand and helped Hetty down with the other. 'How do, Josiah, I shall call you by your given name, since we're almost family. Good to see you again.'

A boy came out and saw to the horse, giving the newcomer a curious look.

Wiping his large, red hand on his apron, Arthur thrust it at Abbs and shook enthusiastically, as though working a pump.

'Capital, let's get you inside. I hope to see plenty of you, now you're here. You've a strong ham inside for your supper and though I say it myself, there's none tastier this side of the county. Step into the shop tomorrow and I'll show you round. Mind you bring him in, Ma.'

'Thank you, I'll look forward to it.'

Charley's son was larger than he recalled. Florid-faced with a resplendent moustache and whiskers, he would be stout by the time he was forty. It was impossible to dislike his friendliness, which was reminiscent of an over-eager dog. Though Abbs suspected a little of him would go a long way and it was strange to hear his sister addressed as *Ma*.

He felt an unkind relief when Hetty explained that Arthur had moved over the shop, he had inherited on his father's death, and did not take his meals with her and Miss Stephens.

'That connects with the shop premises.' She indicated a curtained doorway in her hall, 'but we don't use it any more. It's kept bolted this side. Here's Dora now.' She introduced her assistant, a very pretty young woman, waiting diffidently in the shadows.

Miss Stephens greeted Abbs shyly, enquiring about his journey in a melodious, soft voice. 'It's a great pleasure to meet you at last, Mr. Abbs. Dear Hetty speaks of you so often. We've done everything we can think of to make you comfortable.'

Which had the effect of making him feel the opposite, as he bowed and thanked her. Her cheeks were pink and she looked at Hetty for approval. He knew how shy people often sounded clumsy in their efforts to compensate.

'I'll show you your room and there's time to unpack before supper.' Picking up a lamp, Hetty led the way upstairs.

'We've put you in the back, overlooking the garden. Our bedrooms are at the front here. Downstairs, we use the small parlour by the front door as a sewing-room. That's where I keep all my stock and we show clients in to take fittings. I did think of using the attic but I can't ask older ladies to climb the stairs. The dining-room's opposite and we live in the back parlour. We do much of our work by the fire, this time of year.'

'I'll try not to get under your feet.'

'Josiah, you couldn't. I'm that pleased to have you here.'

Hetty peered earnestly at him and he noticed the red indentation of spectacles, on the bridge of her nose. He recalled a mention in one of her letters, that she needed them for fine work.

'I intended to have all my time free for us but this afternoon, a customer sent word she wants to call in the morning. It's vexing but she isn't one to be put off. There's me longing to make the most of our time together, it is Christmas, after all.'

'Not to worry.' He looked about him appreciatively. 'This is a cosy room, far better than I'm used to.'

'You need someone to look after you.'

'No, really I don't. I'm scarcely there and my evenings are spent reading, same as always. Surroundings don't matter to me, I only meant that you've made all the furnishings.' He glanced round at the plump eiderdown and embroidered pillows. 'You were always good with your needle.'

'Many a pair of breeches I've mended and our Mary's pinafores. Ma couldn't keep up with us all. They were happy days.' Hetty sighed then resumed her usual manner. 'And look at you now, a detective.' She grinned in a way that belied her mature years. 'Come down when you're ready and we'll have some tea.'

~

The first evening had been unexpectedly relaxing, with a generous supper and congenial conversation by the fireside, where Christmas greetings cards filled the mantel-shelf. Hetty showed him a letter of small news and seasonal sentiments from their cousins.

Her home was comfortable and unpretentious, with more space between ornaments than was fashionable. When he'd commented how pleasant it was to sit down without worrying about his elbows, she'd chuckled and said she wasn't a one for endless dusting.

He'd examined a small display of photographs on the bow-legged cabinet from their childhood home, pausing at a study of their mother in old age and passing swiftly over a younger version of himself. It was disconcerting to confront his own image, on view to all in someone else's home.

He'd felt somewhat awkward about staying with a stranger, not wanting to intrude in what was her home, but Miss Stephens seemed most amiable. Fair in colouring, she was eager to please and had a gentle manner.

Abbs was glad to think his sister had such an agreeable assistant. Though Hetty appeared to have made a stoical transition into widowhood, he did not care to think of her being lonely and was aware he could offer no help.

'More toast, Josiah?'

'I couldn't eat another thing, thank you. The rashers were extremely good.'

'We're without a butcher now but the one in Reddenham delivers, that's the next village. Our Christmas goose is hanging in the larder.'

'I noticed the empty shop, next door but one.' Abbs folded his napkin. 'Was that the butcher's?'

Miss Stephens lowered the teapot she was pouring. 'How clumsy of me, fortunately it missed the cloth.' The small splash of tea was confined to her saucer. 'No, that was the druggist's. Sadly, he died about a fortnight ago. An unfortunate accident.'

He realised Hetty was looking at him meaningfully. 'You mentioned you had a customer to see this morning. So I thought I'd take a walk, survey the neighbourhood.'

'The vicar's wife, but she won't call before ten. Let me take you in the shop first, Josiah. Arthur will be offended if we don't look in. He takes great pride in the business.'

'By all means.'

'You're fond of walking, Mr. Abbs?'

Miss Stephens spoke with perfect composure, though he noticed she had abandoned the idea of another cup.

'I am when I get the chance to explore for amusement. I walk most days but that's of necessity, through crowded streets. It's pleasant to be back among open country.'

'It is said that nothing is as agreeable as one's native air,' said Miss Stephens, getting to her feet. 'If you'll excuse me, I'll clear away and set to work. The vicar's wife is rather exacting.' Smiling at Abbs as he rose, she moved gracefully round the table collecting plates.

'What happened to your neighbour?' asked Abbs when they were alone in the scullery. He leant against the wall, Hetty having refused his offer of help. 'You wanted me to change the subject.' He grinned wryly. 'I'd forgotten that expression. You used to do it when we were inattentive in church. You're very like Ma, you know.'

'I do know. I never used to think so but when I take my bed-candle up at night, I catch sight of myself in the glass and see her. Sometimes I hear myself saying the same words she said to us. It's a comfort, somehow.'

Abbs regarded her affectionately. Her wavy hair was still more brown than grey, though she'd grown more rounded in figure and her shoulders were stooped from dressmaking.

'The druggist?' he prompted.

Hetty didn't pause in her swift washing of the breakfast dishes. 'That was terrible. He was knocked down by a train.'

Abbs winced. 'Was he killed outright?'

She nodded as she reached for a tea cloth. 'Mercifully, yes, it was a dreadful tragedy. Bob Fuller was only in his thirties and liked by all. He was walking out with Dora, you see. I doubt it had got as far as an understanding, but anyone could see he was sweet on her.'

'It was an accident then, no possibility of his taking his own life?'

'No one thought so for a moment. He was a young man of happy disposition, with a thriving business.'

'I take it the verdict at the inquest was accidental death?'

Hetty gave him a sharp look, as she dried the teaspoons and rattled them in the drawer of the dresser.

'Yes, of course. The Coroner was perfectly satisfied, Arthur said, and he attended. The vicar would never have buried him in the churchyard if there'd been any doubt. I suppose your profession makes you look for mysteries, where there are none?'

'I dare say,' murmured Abbs. 'Did he fall from the platform?'

'No, there's a crossing place over the railway line on the other side of the village. It's used as a short-cut.' Glancing at the door, Hetty lowered her voice. 'They think he was knocked down there and his body caught up and dragged some yards along the track. They reckoned he was killed instantly, thank the Lord. It doesn't bear imagining.'

'The box that came for Miss Stephens, did it come before or after this Mr. Fuller died?'

Hetty frowned as she dried her hands. 'Before. We'd been to call on an invalid lady who needed a fitting at her house. It was in the porch when we returned.'

Abbs nodded thoughtfully. The modest porch was open at the front and had just sufficient room for one person to open their door in the dry. It had a tiled shelf for deliveries on one side. He'd seen Hetty take a loaf from there earlier.

'I don't suppose you kept the wrapping?'

'Constable Duffield asked that. I usually save brown paper but Dora put it on the fire. All it said was, 'Miss Dora Stephens,' in a printed script. Whoever sent it had taken pains to disguise their hand. I want to forget it. I don't like to think of whoever it was creeping up to the house.' Untying her apron, Hetty dismissed the subject. 'If you're ready, we'll step next door.'

As he helped her on with her mantle, her assistant could be seen at work through the open door of the small parlour.

'I shan't be long, Dora.'

Kneeling, with a tape measure round her neck, Miss Stephens looked up from pinning the hem of a gown. 'Enjoy your walk, Mr. Abbs.'

'You should smile more often, Josiah. You've always a serious look about you. It was the same when you were a small lad.'

Hetty passed through the gate which Abbs was holding open. They paused to let a lady step ahead of them into the grocer's.

A female assistant was arranging boxes of sugared almonds in the window display nearest them. As they entered, she straightened up and bade them good morning in a subdued voice. About Miss Stephens's age, she stood with an awkward air, as if trying to lessen her tall height.

'Good day, Jane,' said Hetty. 'This is my brother who's staying with me.'

She was about to continue when Arthur hurried out from behind the counter and bore down on them.

'Come in, come in, don't mind Jane.'

'That smells tempting.' Abbs inhaled the enticing smell of ground coffee.

'You'll only find best quality here. You must take a packet for him, Ma. No arguments, I insist. Did you sleep well, Josiah?'

'Thank you, yes. Hetty's made me extremely comfortable.'

'Only you're looking pinched, if you don't mind my saying. No offence meant. Smoke-filled cities can't be healthy. Give me fresh country air and a small place where we all know one another. Ain't that right, Ma?'

'I've never lived anywhere bigger than Lynn, so I can't say. Plenty of folk have to move to cities to find work.'

'True, we can't all be fortunate.' Breaking off, Arthur sprang to one side as a customer picked up her basket, ready to leave. 'Allow me, Mrs Thurlow, thanking you for your custom.' Bowing low, he held the door until her trailing skirt was over the threshold.

'Nothing like a fine Stilton for the festive season. What d'you think of my little kingdom? Not that it's so little. Now you saw my pa's old shop, Josiah, what d'you make of this?'

'It looks very well stocked.' Abbs gazed around at the shelves, brimming with ordinary dried goods and Christmas treats.

'You're right there, you won't find better in these parts. But what I meant is *half as big again* as the old premises.' Arthur tapped each finger of his other hand to emphasise his words. Out of the corner of his eye, Abbs saw Hetty stifle a smile. 'I'm delivering further afield every quarter. Excuse me a moment.' Arthur bustled over to the long counter where a lady was deliberating between purchases.

'It means the world to him,' whispered Hetty, a fond note in her voice. 'His father wasn't half as ambitious.'

'It's good to see someone happy in their work. Few people get that, I think.'

'You don't mean yourself?'

He shook his head, touched by her concern. 'Not me, I meant that so many have a life of drudgery to endure.'

The stiff shoulders of the young woman, still occupied at the window, alerted him that his quiet remark had been overheard. Angry with himself, he knew there was nothing he could say to retrieve matters. He had been thinking of the resigned faces he saw in the course of his own work.

Having engaged his customer in discussion, Arthur left the other female assistant weighing biscuits and returned to them.

'Did you see the premises next door are empty, Josiah? A sad business, very sad but after Christmas, I've made up my mind to enquire about taking them on and expanding further.'

Nodding with feigned interest, Abbs saw the young woman, called Jane, look at Arthur with dislike. Her gaze met his for an instant, before she lowered her eyes and returned to neatening the sprigs of holly decorating the boxes.

The customer received her change and the other assistant, small with scraped-back frizzy hair, escorted her to the door. As she left her position behind the polished wooden counter, she had a severe limp.

She greeted them courteously and Hetty introduced him.

'See to the tea, will you, Grace, while there's a lull,' Arthur instructed the young woman.

At first, Abbs thought she was to make tea for the workers, but on following Arthur's suggestion he take a look out the back, he realised his mistake. Behind the shop was a storeroom, filled with bulging sacks and boxes. There, he found Grace dragging a tea chest across the floor, her face etched with painful determination.

'May I give you a hand with that? Please allow me,' he added as she hesitated. 'Over here?'

She nodded shyly and relinquished her hold as he shifted the chest alongside the table, with its scales and paper packets.

'Leave her be, Josiah. She may look as though a puff of wind would blow her over, but Gracie's stronger than you'd think. You mustn't mind her leg,' said Arthur, from the doorway. 'My shop-girls mustn't shirk their share of donkey work.'

'I can manage, Mr. Abbs, thank you.' Grace smiled at him.

He decided he'd had enough of Arthur, though he was as bad with his thoughtless remarks. Thankfully, the bell jangled again as two customers came in together, causing the proprietor to abandon him.

Returning to Hetty, who was conversing with Jane, he waited by her side.

'You and Grace will come and take a glass of punch with us on Christmas Eve, when you shut? I'm sure your parents wouldn't mind this once.' Hetty peered at the younger woman, as though hoping to coax a smile.

She should have been a mother, thought Abbs, or at least a doting aunt and he had failed her in that respect.

'My father doesn't believe in alcoholic drink and levity, Mr. Abbs.' Her eyes were level with his.

'Come for the company.' Hetty pressed her hand. 'It'll only be a few neighbours. You'll know everyone now you've met my brother.'

Jane broke into a smile of real warmth at her kindness. As they left, he thought how it softened her sharp features.

'I feel awful leaving you on your first morning,' said Hetty, as they stood outside the empty shop. 'Our caller won't stay above an hour, you know.'

'Think nothing of it. I'll enjoy stretching my legs after being crammed on trains all yesterday and it's a fine morning.'

Abbs looked in the empty druggist's, as he spoke. The blind was down over the door and he could see nothing of the dim interior, over the wooden screen, behind the single window. The display area had been cleared, apart from a large pestle and mortar. It had a thick layer of dust and contained the body of a dead fly.

Hetty squinted at the cold blue sky. 'Make the most of it, the snow'll be here in a few days.'

'I remember those biting winters of years gone. I've never seen snow elsewhere like we used to get.'

'It's even worse here. I'm glad of the trees at the back, they afford some shelter from the worst of the wind. If you walk towards Lynn, it's pretty enough, but the countryside starts to change in the other direction, nearing the Fens.'

Wrapping her mantle closer, she turned towards the house. 'You'll soon see what I mean. The waterways ice up like sheets of glass in winter. Still, we've plenty of coal and we'll have a cosy Christmas, however many gales howl down the chimney. I'd better go, I'm afraid. I thought we might go to Lynn tomorrow, if you'd care to?'

'I'd like that. I shall see you later.'

They parted and after a few yards, Abbs looked back to find his sister halted at the gate, watching after him. He lifted a hand in farewell, waiting as she turned and went in.

Aylmer was a long, narrow village, set along a by-way that probably led to nowhere in particular, before eventually meandering to King's Lynn. He had read somewhere that his native county was considered to have more villages than any other. This one did not appear as though it had ever been on a coaching route.

The main street contained a handful of businesses and further down, he could see the sign of a second inn, The Barley Mow. One or two passers-by glanced at him. A postman, rummaging in his letter-bag, almost collided with him, as he stepped out of the post office, apologising cheerily and touching his hat.

The church tower, rising behind the cottages, sent him down a lane. Built in Norfolk flint, rather than the local reddish brown carrstone, the church was large for a modest village, bearing witness to the landscape's prosperity in medieval times.

It pleased him to see a flint building again. The carrstone, being confined to the western edge of the county, did not hold the warmth of old memory. In such a churchyard their parents, sister and brothers were buried. The only reason their parents had any memorial was because the squire had offered to provide a stone, having *Head Gardener* inscribed beneath their father's name.

As a raw young constable, he had silently resented his father's life being summed up as someone's servant. The headstone reminded him of the small stones marking the family's dogs, in a gloomy corner of the Hall garden. It was Hetty who had gently pointed out that their mother had been comforted by the gesture.

His brother-in-law's grave was near the gravelled path, a glass dome covering white wax lilies. A placid, kindly widower with a grown son, he'd been quite a lot older than Hetty. She'd taken a post as an assistant-dressmaker in King's Lynn. He suspected she'd thought her chance of marrying had passed, when she made his acquaintance there.

A recently dug grave was marked by a mound of bare earth and a makeshift wooden cross. Abbs thought it ironic that the two former shopkeepers and neighbours lay side by side in death.

The strains of someone playing the organ decided him against looking in the church that morning and he retraced his footsteps.

The imposing vicarage had gateposts surmounted with stone lions. One was missing its head, the broken stump recent, bare of lichen. Beyond the vicarage grounds, the lane petered out in a track leading into the wood.

He wished good day to an old man, pipe clenched between his teeth, pulling a handcart piled with branches and kindling. His steady progress belied his years.

The track ended at a clearing, scattered with torn bark and axe chippings. A fallen trunk had been used as a chopping block and the blackened remains of a fire scarred the ground. Too small to be the work of estate woodsmen, thought Abbs. More likely a pitch for a solitary itinerant. The dispossessed were everywhere.

In any case, the wood was neglected. Fallen trees lay like bowled ninepins, sinking beneath rampant ivy. They would have crashed down in the fierce winds which blew unhindered from the east coast. Hetty had mentioned over supper, that the great house in these parts had been demolished by fire and left ruined.

A thin wood, far longer than broad, it had perhaps been planted originally as a great covert. Few trees remained of considerable age. Apart from the occasional fir and holly, the scene was bereft of colour.

Two paths left the clearing, one leading in the same direction as the village street. Abbs chose the other which soon led to a tumble-down shack, sinking in brambles on the edge of a field. It looked across unremarkable countryside of farmland and sparse hedgerows, with frost glistening on the ridged furrows.

A pigeon burst out of the branches above him, making him start. In the middle of the field, he could see something that resembled a body, but was the remnants of a scarecrow fallen down.

Turning back, Abbs took the other way, at first passing glimpses of the backs of houses on his right. Gradually, he became aware of the distant chug of a train. The sound quickened as he reached a bend and could see the railway line between the edge of the trees.

At once, a great locomotive and carriages roared past, a blank blur of faces and was gone. Leaving only a diminishing hoot and trail of sulphurous smoke. He had found the path across the track, where Hetty's neighbour had been killed.

The last tree was a substantial oak, its bare branches overhanging the edge of the crossing place. As he drew near, something small, placed among its roots, caught his eye. It turned out to be a shrivelled posy. Picking it up, he considered it thoughtfully.

The sort of thing a child might have made and dropped, except it was constructed too carefully. Sprays of holly berries and laurel were bunched together, a plaid ribbon wound round their stems. Tucked in the middle was a faded sprig, which didn't come from the wood. Rubbing it gave off a pungent, almost medicinal aroma, ... *rosemary, that's for remembrance.*

He recognised the ribbon, though that didn't mean anything. If it was sold locally, several women might have purchased a length. It would be interesting to see if a haberdasher were among the village shops.

What it did imply was that someone mourned Bob Fuller and didn't want their identity known. Why else leave it here, instead of on his grave?

Sleepers were laid across the track to indicate a path. A stretch of line was visible for some considerable yards in both directions. There was no obvious reason for someone to have been knocked down. Becoming impatient with himself, Abbs reflected that he was a long way from his jurisdiction. It was no business of his what had or hadn't happened in this village.

Yet it was hard to ignore, when your business was anomalies. There was the matter of the parcel left at Hetty's door. On the face of it, Miss Stephens seemed an unlikely candidate to attract such malice. Unless the motive was jealousy? He made up his mind to watch her and find out the exact nature of the other odd happenings in Aylmer.

A narrow lane began on the far side of the railway line, with two pairs of tied cottages. Coming to a fork, the lane continued in the direction of the station, where he thought it would join the way they had driven on the previous evening.

He chose the other lane, which, after a time, climbed a modest rise between ploughed fields. From his vantage point on the brow, he looked back towards the village and saw what Hetty had meant about its topography.

Behind Aylmer, he could see the beginning of the Fens the railway had traversed, the previous afternoon. Then in the fading light, land and water had begun to merge in horizontal shadows.

On this sharp, bright morning, the land to the south seemed close to black beneath a sparkling skin of frost. He could see several waterways glinting between the bare fields. In the distance, a solitary building stood out, its tall brick chimney puffing black smoke. A steam-pump on the bank of a wide channel.

It was as if the village had turned its back on the bleak emptiness. Setting its face towards a more benign landscape. Hetty appeared contented there, though after Miss Stephens had tactfully retired early, she'd spoken of missing Charley and their old life. He thought it a pity she'd been uprooted from her home in Lynn. They hadn't known it would all be for nothing and Charley dead within a twelvemonth.

After several miles, scarcely aware of how far he'd walked, Abbs decided to go as far as the next church before turning back. Its landmark, round tower rose behind a distant field, still green with winter cabbage.

He sometimes asked himself why he enjoyed wandering round old churches, when he was uncertain of their doctrine. He would attend the Christmas service for Hetty's sake but for the rest, who knew?

He liked reading the memorials with their old names, wondering about the people long gone. The craftsmanship pleased him and the beauty of glass, wood and stone had left something lasting. An antidote perhaps to his work, which was too often about broken things.

At the end of the village, he approached the distinctive shape of a flour-mill, its sails still against the clear sky. Outside the miller's house, Abbs was surprised to recognise Arthur's cart.

A gangling fellow came out of the mill carrying a sack, which he set down by the one already loaded. Arthur followed him, saying goodbye to someone within, his voice carrying across the yard. Looking up he spotted Abbs.

'How do, Josiah. This is well met, I must say. What brings you out here?' Giving no chance to answer, he went on. 'If I'd known you wanted to see these parts, I could have taken you.'

'Good day again. Hetty was expecting a caller, so I thought I'd take a walk.'

'You picked the right way to come unless you fancy striding alongside a dyke, with every chance of getting your boots wet.'

Giving his horse a friendly slap, he climbed on to his seat. 'Hop up and I'll take you back. It's near on time for dinner.'

'I'm obliged to you.'

Now that he had stopped moving, he felt chilled. Despite the sunshine, the day was growing colder.

'Been replenishing my stock, in case we're snowed in,' said Arthur, as they set off. 'As long as folk have the makings of tea and bread, they can manage, I say.'

'Many have to.'

The poor, in the rookeries of his acquaintance, survived on such. Though, without hope of an oven, the bread would be bought. Their loaves would likely be adulterated, the milk watered and the tea would be cheap sweepings from the warehouse floor.

Small wonder they would also add beer to their list of necessities. He did not for a moment think Arthur would 'improve' the flour he sold with alum. Better to be hard up in the countryside than a city.

'We'll soon have you back in the warm.'

He wished irritably that Arthur wouldn't treat him as though he were some elderly invalid, who'd overtaxed himself. He was working out how best to introduce the subject on his mind, when his companion spoke again.

'The truth is I'm glad of this chance of a word, Josiah, while we're on our own. It's about Miss Dora.'

'Go on.' Abbs waited, suddenly guessing what was to come.

'I'm a plain-spoken man, so I hope you won't take it amiss if I ask your opinion of your sister's boarder?'

'She seems most pleasant. I'm glad Hetty has such agreeable company to share her home.'

'Do you ever think of marrying again, Josiah?'

Arthur avoided looking at him as they progressed along the lane. A cart had been drawn up at the edge of a field, where several bent figures were pulling cabbages. A woman straightened up, a hand to her back, watching as they drove past.

'I can't say I do. I'm content enough as I am.'

'Well, I'm not. I dare say that'll surprise you. No, I've reached an age and position where the time's ripe to settle and start a family. Between ourselves, I've a good bit put by and I fancy I've something to offer the right woman.'

'I'm sure you have.'

'It makes sense from every angle. I've given it a lot of thought, never having been one to leap into things. I can provide a comfortable home and I could let one of the shop-girls go.'

Abbs nodded cautiously, wondering which of the two young women Arthur had in mind. There'd been a boy seeing to the horse, presumably his position would be safe.

'I'm glad we understand each other, Josiah. We'll all four have a convivial Christmas.'

'Miss Stephens has no family nearby?'

'She comes from Norwich but she's quite alone in the world. I made it my business to ask.' This was said with a complacent air.

He's pleased there are no dependent relatives to take into account, thought Abbs. He could hear no trace of a Norfolk accent in Miss Stephens's voice, but then it would take a keen ear to detect his. Perhaps she too, had worked on bettering herself.

'Hetty said something about Miss Stephens walking out with your neighbour? She must have been distressed by his death.'

'No more than any of us,' Arthur flicked the reins. 'It's true, Bob Fuller escorted her to a musical evening in Lynn once or twice but she only accepted out of politeness. She's soft-hearted, couldn't hurt his feelings by refusing.'

'What was he like?' asked Abbs, with genuine interest.

'Ingratiating.' When Abbs made no comment, he sought to explain further. 'A shopkeeper must be on good terms with all. But Fuller set out to charm where there was no need.'

'How long had he been in the village?'

Arthur pursed his lips in thought. 'Moved in early last summer. He'd been assistant to a druggist and scraped up the chance to set up on his own, the usual way of things. His coming caused a fluttering in the hen-coop. Not on Miss Dora's part, mind. She's the most fetching young woman in the village and could take her pick. There're few eligible bachelors in Aylmer though.' His expression suggested he was the foremost among them.

'How did the accident come about?'

'He'd been taking medicine to one of the cottages, for Grace's mother. The crippled shop-girl you met earlier. It must have been dusk when he was killed. As I told his friend, when he came to collect his things, if Grace had thought to pick up her mother's pills, Bob Fuller would be alive today.'

'Let's hope she doesn't see it that way.'

Arthur made no answer, intent on steering his horse into the verge for a carrier to pass, its driver touching his hat with his whip.

'Hetty also told me about the pig's head left for Miss Stephens.'

'They were both frightened, a foul trick for someone to play.'

'And not the first?'

Glancing over his shoulder as his load shifted, Arthur set them on their way again. 'There've been a couple of strange things, foolish japes I'd say. But I don't know why anyone would take against Miss Dora. She's obliging in her manner to all.'

'What else has happened?'

'Let me see... one of the vicarage gateposts was smashed. Mrs Craske's hat went missing and was fished out of the village pond. You've seen her too, she was in the shop this morning.'

'It sounds most peculiar,' said Abbs. 'Do all the victims shop with you?'

Arthur laughed, 'I hope you don't think I'm the prankster? There's no one in the village who doesn't get their groceries from me.'

'I wondered if all the victims are female, apart from the vicar?'

'He is a bit of an old woman actually but inoffensive. Now his missus is another matter. Comes from a good family and likes everyone to know she's doing us a favour by being here. I've heard Mrs Merrick reckons this a poor living for her husband. Come to think of it, she had an altercation with Fuller.'

'It's the vicar's wife whom Hetty and Miss Stephens were expecting this morning. What happened with your neighbour?'

Arthur steered the horse round a great pothole before answering, his shoulders hunched against the cold.

'She was purchasing a bottle of cough mixture or something sticky, any rate. As Fuller handed it to her, they dropped it between them and it smashed, splashing some on her skirt. Only a drop or two, I had this from Grace who witnessed it. Mrs Merrick was furious, threatened to sue him for damages and said he'd never get the vicarage custom again.'

Arthur fought a losing battle and smirked. 'Reputation is everything, you know. In a small place like this, that's enough to sink a shopkeeper.'

'Have there been any more strange incidents?'

'I do believe there were one or two things. I have it... a washerwoman's line was kicked down and muddied. You should have a word with our constable, give him a few hints. I'm sure he'd be impressed to meet an inspector with a city force.'

'I shouldn't think so, I used be a village bobby myself. Though I may drop in on him. It sounds like fairly harmless misbehaviour, apart from the pig's head. My concern is for Hetty. I won't have her alarmed by someone's spite.'

'A woman must find it hard to manage without a man's guidance. You know, Josiah, you mustn't worry about your sister. I shall always do my best for her. She was goodness itself to my Pa and a kind, second Ma to me. Arthur Byers doesn't forget what's owed.'

'That's good of you. I know Hetty appreciates your kindness and I'm grateful.'

'That's gratifying, I hope I know my duty. Here we are then, safely back. I dare say you've worked up an appetite?'

They had reached the beginning of Aylmer and were passing a low stone parapet by a large, reed-fringed pond. Arthur slowed as two tired-looking farmworkers shambled across to the Barley Mow and were greeted by a man tethering his horse. Abbs looked at the shops as they went by, a baker's, ironmonger, dairy and a few others. There was no haberdasher among them.

~

The weather had changed overnight. Rain had fallen, loosening the earth and making the day feel unseasonably mild. The sun had been coming out as they left Aylmer. In the town of Lynn, a

22

damp veil of river mist hung between the crowds. It did not lessen the jolly mood of anticipating Christmas and a day off.

A cacophony of sounds met Abbs and Hetty as they made their way through the lower of the two marketplaces, in search of refreshment. Hammering rang out from a boatyard across the river. Gulls screeched, whirling about the masts of fishing vessels and landing on the red tiled roofs.

It was a strange hybrid of a town, thought Abbs, so much of the sea and yet the open waters of the Wash were some distance down the Great Ouse, the final drain of the Fens. Medieval warehouses, built by merchants in the Hanseatic League, were jumbled with elegant townhouses from the last century.

The ancient stone gateway, once defender of the town, was now besieged by new villas, railway tracks diverging to both stations, coal heaps, gasworks and all the unsightly appurtenances of the modern age.

Traders cried their wares from the rows of stalls selling every kind of food, workmen's clothing, trinkets and cheap tin toys. The cobbles were slippery with torn cabbage leaves, discarded bones and fish heads trampled into dung. Small, wiry dogs and the aggressive cold-eyed gulls darted between the townsfolk, warring over scraps.

Abbs took Hetty's arm as he steered them away, keeping a wary eye out for the shabby, sharp-faced children who could snatch and scarper quicker than any creature. They were to be found in any town. A ragged boy squeezed past them, his arms full of the holly and mistletoe he was selling.

The scent of hot chestnuts, roasting on a brazier, drifted along with the plaintive air of a carol being played by an old bugler. On the edge of the marketplace, the alleys down to the quay reeked of tar and the barrel of salted herrings being sold on the corner. The tired suits hung outside the pawnbroker's, still seeming to hold their wearers' shape, were almost brushing the head of the elderly fishwife.

Finally, they reached their destination, a respectable inn by the Corn Exchange.

'It's a treat to see folk enjoying themselves,' said Hetty, when they were seated in the dining-room and the waiter had served

23

their meal. 'I do miss a bit of bustle and there's nothing like the atmosphere in town just before Christmas Eve.'

Her voice sounded wistful, thought Abbs, reaching for the mint sauce. She'd taken a lively interest in the shops and people, making several purchases and enjoying the sight of small children clustered before a display of clockwork monkeys.

'What made Charley move at his time of life? You never really said in your letters.' The instant he'd spoken, Abbs regretted his question. He could guess the answer. The trouble with being a detective was that every conversation sounded like an interview. Being in the police set a man apart.

'You've seen how Arthur's keen to expand. He heard about the shop in Aylmer falling vacant and persuaded his father to take it. We were settled, so I thought, but it was natural Charley should encourage his only son's ambition. And I believe he wanted to make me more secure. He was always aware of the difference in age between us.' Hetty sliced into her chop as she spoke.

'He was a kind man.'

'He was. You know, I look back now and wonder if Charley knew something was wrong. He'd been getting more tired. I think that's how it was. But he didn't really discuss moving with me. Women are sent like parcels where their menfolk require them.'

'Arthur told me how much he values you.'

'He's a good lad. We always got on well. I think it helped that he was a young man when I met his father and he could scarcely remember his ma.'

'Did Charley inherit the staff with the shop?' Abbs speared a boiled potato.

'Yes, Jane and Grace both come from village families. And there's young Matty who runs errands and sees to the horse. Arthur likes to do some of his own deliveries, to the better households. He believes the proprietor's personal service and attention to detail increases custom.'

Their eyes met and the corners of Hetty's mouth twitched. 'Now, Josiah, we mustn't make fun of him. Arthur takes life very seriously. I know he can have a clumsy manner but he means well. That's all that counts.'

Abbs nodded as he ate. In his experience, people who meant well often did a great deal of damage.

'Jane lives with her parents. They're strict Chapel, well, the father is, and he rules the house with a rod of iron. I don't think she and her mother have an easy time. Grace has a sick mother, the widow of a carter. Neither of them have much fun and there's no one for them to meet.'

Arthur had said much the same thing. 'I know a lot of farmhands can't afford to take a wife.'

It had been a little easier in their own village, where work on an estate afforded a degree of security, provided you gave satisfaction.

'They're mostly old in any case. There's Arthur but he's a confirmed bachelor. Young men want something better and they go to the towns.' Hetty sipped from her glass of cider.

Abbs set down his knife and fork, pushing away his plate a little. 'Talking of which, my Chief Constable has suggested I consider applying for a transfer to the Yard. The detective force is expanding with the capital. He's offered to put in a word for me but he needs a decision immediately on my return.'

'Scotland Yard? Move to London?' Hetty stopped eating, her face full of consternation. 'What's brought this on?'

Shrugging, Abbs looked through the dusty window-pane at a poulterer's opposite. A row of rabbit carcasses were hanging on hooks.

'There was a difficult case this autumn. It brought me to his attention, I suppose. He seems to think a move will further my career. My superior hasn't much time for me, perhaps he said something. He'd like to get rid of me, I think.' He smiled wearily at his sister.

'You sound uncertain. Wouldn't Scotland Yard be a promotion?' Hetty watched him anxiously, her food forgotten.

'Not in rank, I'd still be an inspector, but there's a good chance the work would be more interesting.'

'You don't mean more dangerous?'

'Not at all.' Abbs shook his head, striving to look reassuring. 'Don't let your food get cold, Hetty. It's a big decision and I can't afford to make the wrong choice.' As I did once before. The thought lay heavily on his mind. 'The detective-branch of the Metropolitan Police would be a fresh start.'

'I always wondered if you'd move back here some day...' Hetty broke off what she'd been saying, returning absently to her meal.

'Norfolk will always be home in a sense,' said Abbs gently. 'Our part of it, that is,' honesty compelled him to add. 'But there's no going back. I'd rather catch murderers than poachers.'

'I do understand. Will you take this position?'

'I'm still undecided. It was on my mind when I was walking yesterday. Of course, I might not be accepted. If I did go, I'd be nearer Norfolk by the railway. You could come and visit me in London.'

Hetty's face broke into a smile. 'I'd enjoy that.'

~

The police-house was fairly new and situated apart from its semi-detached neighbours, near The White Lion. Dominating the small front garden, the noticeboard stood behind three stiff rose bushes, pruned so severely they might have been standing to attention.

There was no answer at the front door but Abbs could hear someone digging steadily round the back. Following a path at the side of the house, he found himself in a garden all turned over to vegetables, with a rule-straight cinder path down the middle.

A grizzled man, of about Hetty's age, was working there. Despite the time of year, his shirtsleeves were folded back and there was a sheen of sweat on his brow as he straightened up.

'Afternoon, sir. I was wondering if you'd be along to see me.'

The speaker nodded affably at him, no trace of embarrassment at being found attending to his garden in mid-afternoon. Though for all he knew, thought Abbs, the constable had been on duty all night after poachers and was entitled to some time off in lieu.

'Good afternoon. You know who I am, then?' He wasn't impressed but he did approve. A village bobby worth his salt should know everyone on his patch, including any visitors.

'I do that, Inspector Abbs. Ezra Duffield, sir, at your service.'

Waving his hand in a disclaiming manner, Abbs came nearer. 'No need to use my rank here, I'm just paying a family visit for Christmas. Pray don't let me interrupt you.'

Duffield thrust his spade into the tilled ground and looked about him with a satisfied air. 'I reckon the frost'll be back by nightfall. No matter, I'm all but done now. Care to share a pot of tea with me, Mr. Abbs?'

'Thank you, I would.'

He followed his host inside, the constable pausing at the back door to scrape his boots, kicking them on the mat.

'Will here be all right or would you prefer the official room?'

'Here will be fine.'

'Sit yourself down.'

Abbs sat at the table while Duffield stepped into the scullery and was heard swilling water. He was in a kitchen where everything appeared orderly. He could not detect a woman's handiwork. A single gutted fish lay on a tin plate, near a small pan of peeled spuds in water.

The lone, comfortable armchair suggested few visitors were expected. A seed tray filled with bare soil stood on the window sill. It was the room of a man amenable to the bachelor life.

'So this isn't police business, sir?'

Duffield appeared in the doorway, mopping his face with a towel, before lifting his kettle to boil.

'Not as such. As you know, I've no jurisdiction away from my county but I wanted an unofficial word.'

The constable nodded, making no comment as he took china from his dresser and busied himself setting a tray. Some sheets of music were propped by the teapot.

'I'm in the choir.'

Giving the tea a vigorous stir, Duffield spoke with his back to him. He was observant too.

'Always enjoyed a sing-song and when I came here, they were short of baritones. I like the organ,' he added unexpectedly.

'There's some older folk have never taken to it... but all that power, it makes my heart swell.'

'Not for me,' Abbs shook his head at the proffered sugar bowl. 'I'm afraid I'm tone-deaf. I shall be miming at the Christmas service, for the sake of your congregation.'

'Strikes me, the Almighty isn't particular,' said Duffield. 'I've pound cake if you'd like a slice with your tea. My sister makes it.'

'I won't, thanks. I've not long returned from Lynn with my sister. We ate there.'

'I was sorry about your brother-in-law, sir.'

Abbs nodded in acknowledgement. There was nothing he could say. He was painfully aware that the man opposite him probably knew more about Charley Byers's last days than he.

'Terrible mortal thing, cancer. At least it was mercifully quick.'

They sipped their tea, reflecting for a moment.

'How do you find your work here? Do you get much trouble?'

'I needed that.' Draining his cup, Constable Duffield sat back and considered. 'It's a peaceable place when all's said. We did have a spate of ricks and barns being fired in the autumn. That was serious, one caught a farmhouse but luckily no one was injured. The culprit wasn't hard to find. He'd been turned off from one of the farms. I put a nasty bit of work before the magistrates the other week, for cruelty to a horse. No excuse for that.'

Abbs grimaced. 'I see it too. You'd think country folk would look after their animals but I know it doesn't follow.'

'You and Mrs Byers are from the north of the county, I believe?'

'That's right.' Abbs mentioned the market town where he'd first joined the county police.

'What can I do for you, Mr. Abbs?'

'My sister spoke of some odd incidents in the village of late. I wanted to ask you about them.'

'Odd's the word. They're just mischief for the most part. Small beer but I don't like it. Small misdemeanours unchecked have a habit of leading to worse.'

'I agree. Do you mind going through them with me? Arthur Byers told me one or two, but he thought there were more.'

28

'I'd be glad to talk it over. What did Arthur have to say?'

Abbs repeated what he'd been told while Duffield replenished their cups. 'My first thought about the vicarage gatepost was a small boy with a catapult.'

'And mine. Funnily enough, it must have been smashed during school hours. There aren't that many young 'uns in the village and they walk to the school at Reddenham, three miles away. I checked with the schoolmaster. They were all accounted for that day.'

Thorough, Abbs noted with approval. 'It's a quiet lane. I went down there yesterday. No houses beyond the vicarage, not overlooked.'

'I happened to see you, sir, in the churchyard.'

'You clearly don't miss much, Constable.'

Duffield grinned. 'Just doing my rounds. There was a pile of stones lying nearby when the incident took place, ready for filling in potholes. Ammunition in plenty and one good throw would have done it. Easy as a coconut shy.'

Taking a cautious sip, Abbs pictured the scene as Duffield spoke again.

'Something you won't have heard about was a curious theft from the home of Mr. Robert Fuller, lately deceased.'

'What was taken?'

'Very little. Mr. Fuller was the chemist here. He'd gone to town on early closing afternoon. While he was out, someone purloined his best jacket and new billycock. I say it was no ordinary burglary, for nothing else was taken. He'd left his rent money in an envelope on the mantelpiece.' Duffield fingered his whiskers as he watched his guest's reaction.

'That's certainly strange. It could have been a vagrant, I suppose. Any food missing?'

Duffield shook his head. 'Funny you should say that, Mr. Abbs. I did have occasion to collar a vagrant a week later. He'd been sleeping in someone's hen-house and he was wearing the stolen items. When I questioned him, turned out he could prove he'd been in Lincolnshire at the time they must have been removed. He'd had a day's spud-lifting there. He was making his way down here. Swore blind he'd found the hat and jacket in a field on the edge of the village.' He paused to swallow his tea. 'Said he saw them on a scarecrow.'

Abbs's eyebrows rose. 'Someone had it in for Mr. Fuller then.'

'And not just him. Know what I think, sir?'

'I'd like to hear your theory.'

'It strikes me there's an unhappy woman behind it. There was a lady's hat got ripped and chucked in the pond as well. And a clothes line knocked down, the washing trampled in puddles. What man would think of ruining clothes? That's female malice.'

'Sound reasoning. Tell me, do you think these incidents have stopped?'

'Hard to say, sir.' Duffield poured himself a third cup. 'No one's told me of anything lately.'

Abbs declined the proffered teapot. 'Do you have anyone in mind for the culprit?'

The constable hesitated, applying himself to stirring his sugar, in tea the colour of leather.

'I've an idea but I can't confront anyone without proof. If I'm right - and this is only based on a look I caught - there's no real bad in her. But it's my duty, I know, to have a word in her ear. Can't overlook someone breaking the law, just because they're unhappy.'

'No, indeed.'

He raised his eyes, giving Abbs a searching look. 'It needs nipping in the bud before she does something that can't be put right. But we've still got to live together. It's too small a place to have someone avoiding me ever after. People would notice and wonder. She'd feel she had to leave and Lord knows what that might lead to. Not something I'd want on my conscience.'

Duffield sat back with the air of a man who'd said his piece and no more.

'I do see your dilemma,' said Abbs. He saw that he was reliant on the constable's goodwill and not in a position to push him. 'You know your own people. My concern is for my sister. Whoever sent the pig's head didn't care about her fright. I know it was intended for Miss Stephens, but even so.'

Duffield nodded unhappily. 'I shouldn't think anyone would want to upset Mrs Byers. I did enquire of the nearest butcher's, if anyone from here had purchased a pig's head, but it was hopeless. Plenty of women like to make their own brawn.'

'What about Miss Stephens?'

The constable's tea cup looked fragile in his large hands, thought Abbs as he watched him look down. Despite his size, he's a gentle soul. On the way indoors, Duffield had paused to move a snail out of harm's way. He could imagine those thick fingers carefully handling his vegetable seedlings.

'Would anyone want to upset her?'

'You know what women can be like when they're jealous.'

'Have there been any incidents since Mr. Fuller's death?'

'Not to my knowledge. Are you thinking they're connected?'

Abbs told him about the posy he'd found by the railway crossing. 'It hadn't been there more than a few days. I'd seen a young woman wearing a similar ribbon a short time earlier. Hardly conclusive, I admit, but what do we have? An unknown woman who mourns Mr. Fuller and an unpleasant trick played on a woman he was courting. It does sound like a case of jealousy.'

'There's something else about the parcel you should know. A fellow as lives opposite Mrs Byers was working outside that morning. Doing a few jobs on his house before winter. He saw the ladies leave. What he didn't see was anyone leave a package. He was there the whole time until they returned home. Clearing his guttering, hanging his gate and no one came.'

Regarding him thoughtfully, Abbs took a moment to reply. 'The implications of that are worrying. Your suspect seems to make a habit of entering other people's properties.'

'Of course, Henry can't literally have been looking every minute. He had to turn his back at times to do his work.'

'But not long enough for someone to have opened Hetty's gate, stepped on a tile path and deposited a parcel in the porch?'

'No. He's adamant he didn't go inside. The ladies weren't away that long.'

Abbs ran a hand through his nondescript brown hair, thinking vaguely that he must call in a barbershop before reporting back on duty.

'Then it must have been left from inside. It would only take a few seconds to cautiously open the front door and push out a parcel. My sister was very disturbed by it and Miss Stephens even more so, I should think. I haven't spoken of this with her.'

'How would you tackle this, Mr. Abbs? I might be wronging someone completely innocent.'

'I'd work out when the incidents started,' he replied slowly. 'Then I'd look at the village and ask myself what changed. There must have been a catalyst.'

'That's much what I did, if not in those words.'

'And?'

The constable collected their saucers and removed the tray before returning to the table. A patient man, Abbs waited until he was ready to speak.

'Bob Fuller settled in the village a couple of months before they started.' There was still a reluctance to be detected in his tone. 'That's all I can see that changed. Nothing much happens in a small place like this. A stranger can stir things up without meaning to, or even knowing.'

Abbs recalled what Arthur had said on the previous day. 'You mean among women who perhaps thought their chance of marrying had gone by?'

'Women liked him,' said Duffield simply. 'I don't think he set out to make himself regarded. He had an amiable manner to everyone, including men. Charm, I suppose you'd call it. A rare quality that can wreak havoc.'

Two

The bedroom felt much colder. Abbs could see, in the moonlight, that Constable Duffield had known his weather. Frost had returned to their corner of Norfolk. Woken by the dying chimes of the church clock, he had been unable to sleep again and lighting his candle, lay reading for a time. Concentration had proved elusive. Wrapping himself in his eiderdown he had moved to the window-seat, his bare feet chilled on the painted floorboards beyond the carpet.

He sat looking out at the indistinct, mysterious shapes that slowly resolved into wall, bush, tree-tops, coal-house roof. To his left, ran a row of gardens, Hetty's being the last. Beyond her house, the rear of the shop premises was a workmanlike yard with various small out-houses. Unlike the house, no access had been made in the wall between the two.

The gardens had gates on to a rear path, running the length of the terrace. He now knew that an old wall separated the path from the wood. In poor repair, it had tumbled down in several places. Doubtless, some stone had been appropriated for the building of rockeries.

Constable Duffield had told him that, as he'd guessed, the wood was not keepered. The owners lived elsewhere after the Hall was burned down. The farms were let and the agent was at Reddenham. It would have been easy for someone who dared to sneak unseen in these houses, then vanish in the wood.

Though in this house, there was another way. The frost had traced spider-work patterns on the edge of the glass. On impulse, Abbs pushed open the casement to feel the cold. An uneven row of icicles hung from the gutter. The air was as fresh and clean as pegged washing.

An idea had occurred to him. Dressing swiftly, he wanted to put it to the test without being seen. Hetty had a lot to do, with her guests coming. She was sure to be down shortly to lay the fires.

He crept down the stairs, avoiding the treads near the top that creaked and the loose stair rod. The tick of the long-case clock sounded unnaturally loud as he reached the hall.

The leeks which Duffield had presented to him, wrapped in a news-sheet, had been boiled with supper. Their smell faintly lingered. Moving cautiously, Abbs went to the thick curtain which hid the connecting door to Arthur's premises. Easing it back, he saw the bolt below the finger-plate. It was undrawn.

Turning the knob, he edged the door open a crack and listened. Silence, no sign of Arthur stirring. Glancing back up the stairs, he opened the door further, very slowly, alert all the time for a betraying sound from wood or hinge.

Stepping through, he found he was in a short passage with a door on either side and the hall directly ahead. The arrangements did not mirror Hetty's side, as it was a larger house and built as shop premises. The door to the left was not pulled to.

Stepping a few paces forward, he glanced in a kitchen. A smeared knife lay on a bread board, with a flower-patterned cheese-dish alongside. It looked familiar, the evening snack of a man who wanted swift sustenance, without crockery to wash up.

The other door was shut. He listened again before opening it by inches, all the while watching Arthur's hall. As expected, it was the storeroom, tainted with an odour of stale spices, ginger and something else. The dark interior was illumined only by a casement, high up on the wall, that borrowed light from the shop.

He didn't know what he expected. No answer was to be found among the sacks of rice and sugar, the broom propped in a corner. He and the local man had reached the same conclusion but there was no proof. What, if anything, should he do?

If it were simply a question of a foolish young woman's hysteria, he would leave matters to Duffield. But he couldn't shake off a suspicion that something far darker was at work.

His boot nudged against a faint chink of metal, an empty mousetrap. His heart thudding, Abbs retreated. It would be hideously embarrassing to be caught in Arthur's home. Safely by the connecting door, he listened again. Nothing.

Though there was a something in the silence. A kind of *denseness* in the air that said, beyond all rational knowing, the house was occupied. That feeling was never wrong. Every housebreaker knew it. It had once saved his life, in a supposedly empty crib, in the heart of a rookery.

Safely back in his sister's house, Abbs gently shot the bolt behind him. If someone had entered Hetty's house from the shop, they would not come through a second time. Something warm brushed against his legs.

Stifling an exclamation, he looked down to see Hetty's cat, Smut, weaving in small circles and staring blandly up at him with goosegog eyes. They had made friends on the night he arrived.

Replacing the curtain folds, he carried him into the scullery and carefully set him down. Smut stalked determinedly to the back door, tail erect and he let him out. After hunting for the match-safe and lighting the range, he went into the parlour and let in the dawn.

The first glimmerings of sunrise were a livid pinkish-red, like the blood beneath the surface of a bruise. It was, as every school-boy knew, a warning sky. He thought about Hetty saying that the connecting door was kept bolted and never used since Charley's death.

Knowing her amiable nature, he had no doubt that Arthur's assistants had been invited in at some time. There would have been messages and groceries carried round from the shop. Easy enough to be alone in the hall for a few seconds and draw the bolt behind the curtain, knowing it wouldn't be seen.

'It looks very festive, does it not?' said a soft voice.

Abbs spun round with an inner jolt. His hearing was keen yet he hadn't heard Miss Stephens descend the stairs. With an effort, he brought his thoughts to their surroundings and agreed.

They had decorated the tree before supper. That is, the two women had busied themselves enthusiastically. He had mostly read on the sofa. Smut had been banished from the room after trying to pat the glass baubles on the lower branches.

Plaid ribbon bows, crackers, sweets in screws of bright paper, fir cones and candles were crammed about the tree, which was crowned with a bisque angel. The mantel shelf and picture rail were hung with laurel and ivy, with sprigs of bright holly berries at intervals. He was only glad there was no mistletoe bough.

On the sideboard, pedestal bowls of ruby glass held pyramids of pears, filberts, oranges and crystallised fruits. The tantalus was dark with brandy and sherry. A pressed glass punch-bowl, with its ladle and hanging cups, stood ready to be filled.

'I dare say it recalls happy childhood memories for you and your sister?'

'It does. Hetty always dressed the tree with our mother and our younger sister. I expect she's told you our father was a gardener? He would cut greenery from the estate and the wood ranger used to bring us a yule log, always apple for the scent. They spit fiercely and we'd have to snatch our chestnuts from the hearth, dodging the sparks.'

'I never saw such a sight. I was raised in an orphanage.' Miss Stephens continued to gaze at the tree.

It seemed kinder to remain silent, than murmur a conventional expression of sympathy but he couldn't ignore her.

'You moved from Norwich, I believe? Is that where you grew up?'

'It is.' There had been a faint hesitation. 'They taught me to sew at the orphanage and that has served me well.' She turned to him with her usual composure. 'You are down very early, Mr. Abbs. I trust you didn't have a disturbed night?'

'I woke and couldn't get back to sleep.'

'You must have a great deal on your mind. I understand you are off to London in the new year?'

Standing demurely with her hands clasped, Miss Stephens looked as neat as a doll, even at that hour. It was impossible to imagine her soft hair in rags, as it must have been.

He felt a spurt of irritation at Hetty. It hadn't occurred to him to ask her to keep their conversation to herself.

'Nothing is settled. It's simply a possibility.'

Miss Stephens put her head on one side as she smiled at him. 'I'm sure it will be a great advancement for you. Though you'll find London a vast and lonely place, without any acquaintance there.'

He was relieved to hear Hetty on the stairs and opened the door to avoid answering. Unlike her companion, she was still reaching back to thrust a pin in her chignon and smooth a few stray wisps, as she greeted them.

'Straight after breakfast, I shall set to work baking the mince pies. You can keep me company, Josiah. You'll see to the punch and prepare the negus, Dora? You've such a tidy way of slicing fruit.'

'Gladly. And anything else you wish me to do.'

'Bless you, my dear. I do love Christmas. After last year... Well, we must all count our blessings and look to the future.'

They followed as she bustled into the kitchen and tied her apron over her skirt. Miss Stephens began collecting china. Her deft, economical movements were in contrast to Hetty's darting about, seeing to several things at once.

'Is there anything I can do today? I could see to the fires.'

'Would you really? That would be a help. If you could see the coal scuttles are kept filled this afternoon. There are some logs by the wash-house. We might need someone to fetch anything I've forgotten, before the shops close early.'

'Your poor brother will think we mean to work him to death.' Miss Stephens made a mock protesting face at him. 'If you would just get the door for me, Mr. Abbs.'

'Let me carry that for you.'

Taking the tray, he followed her in the front room. There was a slightly awkward silence, which he did not feel disposed to fill. Miss Stephens laid the table, her head bent to her task.

~

Hetty's neighbours were most affable, though Abbs felt the presence of a policeman tended to inhibit any social gathering. Matters were not helped by Arthur's displaying him from person to person, as though he was an exhibit in a menagerie.

Wearing his best frock coat, Arthur had taken up a proprietorial stance by the sideboard, dispensing glasses of negus and good cheer in equal measure. He had looked in during the morning, presenting Hetty with a dented tin of Huntley's Christmas biscuits and several boxes of sticky figs. Over-ordered stock it was too late to shift, thought Abbs uncharitably.

Hetty was in her element, making sure everyone was helped to food and conversation, with no one overlooked. Grace and Jane had appeared in Arthur's wake when he'd finally shut up shop for the holiday. Only the errand boy was absent. He knew his sister had sent him off with a box of treats for his family.

When Constable Duffield arrived, his hair slicked down with macassar oil, Abbs waited while he was greeted by everyone present and supplied with a warming glass. Before he could catch the constable's eye, he was waylaid to give his opinion, as a detective, on the likely outcome of the Tichborne trial.

It was some considerable time later when he managed to get Duffield out of earshot. Under the pretext of showing him Hetty's garden, before the light failed.

'Very pleasant spot in summer, I should think. I mind Mr. Byers senior had this made when they first came. Before he was taken ill.' Duffield was examining a trellis-arbour with a bench inside. 'Do you happen to know what the rose is, Mr. Abbs?'

'No idea, I dare say my sister will remember. I've..'

'It was very good of Mrs Byers to invite me.'

'Never mind about that. I've found something which seems to confirm your suspect.' Abbs recounted his discovery.

Duffield shook his head sadly when he'd finished. 'That settles it then. One of us will have to have a word. She needs to be brought to her senses, before there's a criminal charge to be laid.'

'One of us? This isn't my village, Constable.'

'It would come better from you, sir, being an outsider.' Duffield regarded Abbs steadily. 'I'm not known for shirking my duty, though you've only my word on that, but it seems to me for the best.'

'Because you both have to live here.' Abbs sighed. 'Very well, Constable. I know when I'm beaten.'

Duffield broke into a warm smile. 'I'm grateful to you, Mr. Abbs.'

Turning away to hide his amusement, Abbs faced the apple tree in the small lawn. 'How I shall contrive the opportunity, I don't know,' he muttered.

'If there's anything I can do in return?'

'You could tell me all you know about Robert Fuller's death. When were you called out that night?'

Cold as he was, Abbs listened intently as Duffield related the events of the body's discovery and the inquest. From time to time, he asked a pertinent question.

'I'm obliged to you. We'd better get in before Hetty sends out a search party.'

They made their way back to the house, treading with care as the frost had scarcely retreated all day.

Abbs halted at the kitchen door. 'I could have sworn I shut that behind me.' He distinctly recalled turning the brass knob, so as not to let the cold in. The door was now ajar.

Inside, the door mat was slightly skewed, as though someone had stepped back hastily.

Returning to the parlour, Abbs ran his eye casually over the guests. Everyone looked as though they'd been conversing happily for some time. The folding doors between front and back parlour had been opened, for the purpose of accommodating the guests.

He wandered over to Grace, who was by herself in the smaller room at the front, where they took their meals. She was reading the titles of the volumes in a bookcase. He recognised the ploy of someone feeling awkward at a gathering. Though she was studying the spines with what appeared to be genuine interest. She looked up with a shy smile as he joined her.

'You enjoy reading, Miss Tillson?'

'Books are my escape from daily cares, Mr. Abbs. That is to say, novels are. I'm afraid I'm not clever enough to read studious works.'

'You do yourself an injustice. After a long day, I'd much rather lose myself in a world of someone's imagining than study.'

'Mrs Byers is fond of reading, I know. She's been very kind in lending books to my mother. We had another neighbour who did likewise.' Grace looked down, her expression pensive. 'You have perhaps heard about the death of Mr. Fuller, who kept the shop on the corner?'

Abbs nodded soberly. 'My sister told me of the accident. A terrible business.'

He kept his voice discreet, though apart from two old ladies intent on their sherry and gossip, the greater part of the company were at the other end of the room.

'It was such a shock, Mr. Abbs.' Glancing at the others she lowered her voice almost to a whisper. 'When it happened, Mr. Fuller was on his way home from our house. My mother and I almost felt some blame attached to us.'

'That cannot possibly be so, Miss Tillson. It's human nature to look for cause. But I hope reflection has made you see that it was nothing to do with you.' He spoke with conviction, mindful of Arthur's remark. Mr. Fuller had been delivering medicine that Grace could have collected.

She gave a small nod, her face pale beyond the lamplight. 'My mother is an invalid, you see and doesn't often get out. Mr. Fuller would make up her pills for me. Once he got to know us, he fell into the habit of calling in and taking a dish of tea with her. His conversation always did her good. He used to make us laugh, Jane and me. We saw a lot of him with our workplace being next door.'

As she finished speaking, Grace winced, shifting slightly to ease her hip.

'Shall we sit down, Miss Tillson?' Abbs drew out a chair for her, pausing while she arranged her skirt. 'May I fetch you some refreshment?'

'Thank you, some fruit cup, if you please.'

'It's good of you to talk to Grace.' Hetty smiled at him as he reached her side. 'She's a quiet little thing. Is she all right?' She peered across the room.

'Only fatigued I think. It must be hard on her to stand for hours.'

'She isn't one to complain.' Another guest claimed her before she could say more.

'I'm sorry you and Mrs Tillson have lost a friend,' said Abbs, taking a seat by Grace.

'You're very kind.' She tried her punch and they sat in companionable silence.

Life's a chancy business, thought Abbs. There's someone like part of the furniture. Their company valued but taken for granted. Everyone's busy, no time to stop and reflect. Suddenly they're gone. Never to be seen again in this world.

Too late, alas, to say anything you meant to. Too late to ask the questions you were going to one day. How quickly they become a description in a reminiscent voice.

'You are here a few more days, I think, Mr. Abbs?' Grace looked hesitantly up at him.

'Yes, though I must leave before the year ends.'

'I wonder if I might ask you a great favour?'

'Yes, of course. If I can aid you in any way?' She had succeeded in surprising him.

'Mrs Byers often sits with my mother. Might she bring you along to meet her? My mother would so enjoy seeing a new face. She's heard all about your visit.'

'Why, certainly. I'd enjoy meeting Mrs Tillson very much.'

She looked so strung with nerves, he hadn't the heart to make an excuse. In truth, he was always interested in people. He would be able to think of Hetty in her world when he was far away. Wherever that would be.

Darkness had fallen by the time people began to take their leave. Handshakes were exchanged, Christmas greetings and many hearty expressions of goodwill among neighbours who, for the most part, would be seeing one another shortly at the midnight service.

Arthur stood with Hetty to see them out. Very much as though he were owner of the house. Miss Stephens busied herself in fetching coats and shawls, smiling graciously, holding out scarves and mufflers. Watching her, Abbs decided she was the pattern of a perfect companion, never putting a dainty slipper wrong.

Lanterns were lit and folk set off, amid called warnings to be careful for the ground was freezing. Grace left, after thanking him again, in the company of an elderly farmer and his wife. They were taking her home in their cart. He guessed the old man had employed her father and owned the cottage where they lived.

'Josiah, would you mind turning out into the cold?' Hetty appeared at his elbow. 'Could you offer Jane your arm and light her way home? She lives down a lane at the far end of the main street.'

'By all means.'

He accompanied her across the room. Jane was waiting by the door, holding her mantle and scowling.

Hetty saw them out, handing Abbs a lantern and the two of them set off in silence. He looked up at the pinprick stars in a dark sky that seemed infinitely remote. At his side, Jane craned her neck, following his gaze.

'Sorry about this,' she said abruptly. 'I could manage by myself.'

'It's no trouble, Miss Goddard. I rather like being out at nightfall.' He felt her eyes assessing him as they turned into the main street.

'I rarely get the chance to go out in the evening.'

He waited but no more was forthcoming. Two of the guests who'd left just ahead of them, called goodnight to their companion and halted at a door between shops. Fumbling with a key, the husband ushered his wife inside, the other fellow moving further into the dark. His heels rang out, gradually dying away, leaving them alone in the street.

They passed the shop windows, each with their seasonal greetings card from the proprietor, thanking everyone for their custom. Predictably, Arthur's had been the most ostentatious.

Lamplight glowed from the baker's, where they would be busily preparing for the morrow. In the stationer's, their *A Merry Christmas To One And All* banner looked forlorn, already hanging down at one edge.

'Are you looking forward to a day off, Miss Goddard?'

Jane shrugged indifferently beside him. 'Christmas day is much like any other in our house.'

'Steady.' Abbs grasped her arm just below the elbow, as her foot slid on a dark sheen of ice. Her mantle felt too thin for winter.

'Oh, thank you, Mr Abbs. I didn't see it.'

'My fault for not lighting your way better. It's where the shopkeeper emptied his bucket this morning, I expect.'

Her expression softening, Jane decided to unbend a little. 'We'll be at the chapel service tomorrow. There's just me and my parents at home. We'll have a goose and in the afternoon my father will give us Bible readings. Some of the Elders are coming to tea. That's it really. Might as well be at the shop, only you'll have Arthur tomorrow.' She gave him a wry smile as they set off again.

'Have you always lived here?'

'I'm never likely to leave. My parents are content here. My father's clerk to a seed merchant but the chapel is his life.'

'And you don't share that?' Abbs glanced curiously at her as they walked. He had not proffered his arm, guessing she would prefer to walk independently. Instead, he held the lantern above her path and waited for an opening.

Jane shook her head. They walked in silence along the street, past the lane leading to the church.

In a few hours, its door would be thrown open. The interior would be full of flickering candlelight and warmly wrapped villagers. Constable Duffield would be among the choir. He and Hetty would see Christmas in together as they had done in their youth.

A dog barked in one of the cottages, then, their echoing footsteps apart, the evening was silent again. He had forgotten how dark it could be without gas-lamps. It made the time seem much later than it was.

'It isn't much further.' She sounded almost reluctant to go home.

When they reached the pond, they both slowed. As people generally do where there is water to be looked at. Setting the lantern carefully on the parapet, Abbs glanced across at the nearby inn. A sliver of light glowed feebly where the curtains met. No one was abroad.

'There are ducks here in the summer.' Leaning forward, Jane gazed at the still water. 'It's starting to freeze but it will take a week before the ice will bear weight. Folk will be skating on the Fens by January. It's hard to believe summer will ever come again.'

He wondered if she was only referring to the winter. He retrieved the woman's name from his memory. 'Was it from here you threw Mrs Craske's hat in?'

His words sank in like a stone lobbed in the water. He heard her intake of breath. Her frightened face stared at him. She didn't reply, remaining still, hands braced on the stonework. A neat darn disfigured one of her gloves.

A shaft of pity made him wonder how he found himself in this position. For Hetty's sake, he thought.

'Who told you? Who else knows?' Her voice was dull with resignation.

'No one,' some instinct made him say. 'My sister and Arthur told me what's been going on here. I guessed it was you.'

She didn't ask how. 'Are you going to arrest me?' Shivering, she hugged her arms across herself, looking down at the water.

'No,' said Abbs, freeing himself from his warm travelling-coat. 'I have no authority here, even if I wanted to, which I don't. We can sort this out now. Your parents won't be anxious if you're a few minutes longer?' She shook her head. 'Here, take this. Go on, I insist. No sense in catching a chill.'

Wan with misery, she draped the heavy cloth about her shoulders and waited like a cornered animal.

'So what had this Mrs Craske done to upset you?'

'I was angry with her. She made fun of Grace, about her limp.'

'How did you come by her hat, anyway?'

'She'd painted it and left it to dry by an open window. I had to deliver an order for the house next door. When I saw it there, I thought it would serve her right.'

In spite of himself, Abbs suppressed a smile. She sounded like a small girl. 'What about the vicar's wife?'

Huddling herself deeper into his coat, Jane continued. 'She gave someone the sharp edge of her tongue.'

'It was a good shot, worthy of a bowler.'

'My brother taught me how to throw and catch when I was a girl.'

'Your brother?' He didn't ask further in case he lay in the churchyard.

'Michael. He isn't dead that we know of, but he might as well be. He doesn't ever write. He ran away years ago, leaving a note that said he was off to sea. We had one short letter addressed to Ma, then no more. He didn't get on with our father.'

Abbs thought of the years in which he had grown apart from Hetty, the scrappy letters, one to her lengthy three. There had never been any loss of affection. Ten years difference in age, a geographical distance and the business of living was enough to divide them.

'You realise this was criminal damage?' He spoke mildly. 'You can't go around breaking the law, however justified your anger feels at the time. Some people have cruel tongues and you must school yourself to ignore them.'

'I know you're right, Mr. Abbs. I shouldn't have smashed her precious gatepost, but you don't know how vicious Mrs Merrick can be. She hasn't imbibed much of her husband's teachings and he just parrots what any clergyman should say. At least, at chapel they mean it. She was vile to... to someone I cared about.'

'Mr. Fuller?'

Jane twisted towards him, her face, above the lantern, a white mask of dismay. 'Does everyone know?'

'No one, as far as I'm aware. It's my job to work things out. By making connections,' he added.

'How did you find out?' she whispered.

'I came across the posy you left by the railway crossing. It was you?' She nodded. 'It was pure chance. I followed the path along the edge of the wood, directly after I met you and Miss Tillson in the shop. I recognised the ribbon tying the stems, the same as you were wearing. I couldn't be sure you'd placed it there. But when I found that no shop in Aylmer sells ribbon, it seemed likely.'

There was a short silence while she appeared to think over his words. Abbs realised he was numb with cold, though it was unimportant.

'Have you told your sister or the constable?'

'No one else,' he lied. 'Your secret is safe with me, provided I have your word there'll be no more tricks played and particularly no house-breaking. I heard about Mr. Fuller's jacket ending up on a scarecrow. You must see such behaviour is madness. You could end up in gaol.'

'I know that, I do.' She hung her head, drooping over the parapet until he feared he'd have to restrain her. 'You have my word on it, sir. Please don't tell anyone, I couldn't bear it. I'd do away with myself, however much it's a sin.'

'Compose yourself, Miss Goddard. Someone may come along.' He spoke rapidly, keeping his voice low. 'We've all done things we regret. I accept your assurance. You have my word that I'll recount this conversation to no one.'

Nor would he in detail, though Duffield would have to know the matter was resolved.

She raised her head, gazing at him bleakly, her eyes brimming. 'You speak of madness. I know I did a terrible thing to go into Bob's house. My parents would die of shame if they knew. They'd want no more to do with me. And my father would take his belt to me first. You were right, I was a little insane, I think. I felt so wretched and angry.'

'What made you do it?'

'I wanted to hurt him and stop him taking Dora Stephens to another concert. I could see she wanted him from the first. I thought if I spoilt his good attire, he couldn't go. When I had his things, all I could think of was getting out of there. I was too frightened to keep them so I was going to hide them in an old shack by the wood. But then I saw old Farmer Turl's scarecrow lying down. I didn't know what I was doing.'

Abbs gestured to hush her as a man came into sight, walking towards them. It wouldn't do to be seen talking together in the dark. Fortunately, the fellow was busy watching his boots as he crossed the yard before the inn. Pausing only to spit copiously, he disappeared beneath the porch. He heard a snatch of piano music, abruptly snuffed out.

'I wanted to see how he lived. Dora Stephens didn't care for him, not in the way I did. I would have worked all hours for Bob, scrubbed his floors, helped him build up his business. He needed someone to look after him. But what man would ever want to marry a plain beanpole like me?'

It was painful to hear the despair in her voice. What could he say to console her, without making matters worse? Abbs thought back to someone he'd met that autumn. Someone who'd seemed quite unremarkable, at first. Yet somehow, she had become less ordinary on each subsequent meeting.

'Don't try to be kind, Mr. Abbs. D'you know what your Arthur calls us, Grace and me? Plain Jane and clumsy Grace. He thinks that's witty. It amuses him no end.'

'Then he's an ignorant fool,' said Abbs.

Producing a handkerchief from her skirt, Jane began wiping her eyes at last.

'Is there no woman you could confide in, your mother or a friend?'

'No. My mother would be horrified. Grace is nice enough, but we don't speak about private things. I like your sister, she's always treated me well but I couldn't talk to her. She's Miss Stephens's friend.'

'Whatever you think of Miss Stephens, she didn't deserve the pig's head. And sneaking into my sister's home, to leave it on the doorstep, is a poor way of repaying her kindness.'

'But I didn't. Why ever would you think that?' Bunching the wet scrap of cotton in her glove, Jane looked aghast. 'I didn't send anything to Miss Stephens. And I've never been in Mrs Byers's house without her asking me in.'

Abbs gazed thoughtfully at her. 'Have you ever been through the connecting door between my sister's house and the shop?'

'Once or twice when Mr. Byers senior told me to.'

'Not since then?'

'No, I swear. I know I went into Bob's house, which I shouldn't have done, but I'd never do anything to hurt your sister. She's always treated me as an equal. I don't like Dora Stephens but I didn't send her a pig's head. I didn't trample Mrs Corman's washing either. It must have blown down. Please don't turn me in... I wish I could make you believe me.'

'I rather think you have.' Abbs glanced along the street. Hetty would be wondering if he'd lost his way. 'Come along, Miss Goddard. Try to put all this behind you now. It's Christmas Eve and it's been a long day for you, I don't doubt. Let us get you home.'

~

'There's nothing like a ghost story on Christmas night, when we're all cosy round the hearth. Will you read to us, Josiah? You've a soothing voice.'

'If I must, though I feel too idle to move.' Recalled to his surroundings, Abbs sat up straighter and took the book from his sister. Rather ungraciously, he turned to the index. 'Which is it to be?'

Glad though he was to be in company with Hetty, Christmas Day had seemed interminable. He had lain awake the night before, mulling over his conversation with Jane Goddard. If she hadn't left the pig's head parcel for Miss Stephens, then who did? Her vehement denial had carried the unmistakable ring of truth. He'd felt there'd been a premeditated spitefulness about it. Whereas, everything Jane had owned up to doing had been impulsive.

She'd obviously been living under great strain, finding a relief in making a clean breast of her misdemeanours. They'd spent a few moments more, just out of sight of her parents' windows, while she composed herself and thanked him. He'd done his best to convince her to make a fresh beginning, and thought he'd succeeded.

She'd seemed calmer when he watched her go in. Women were fortunate, he reflected, that they had recourse to tears. It seemed that once they gave way, their worst misery was washed away with the salt, leaving them with a new resolution.

He and Hetty had discreetly exchanged gifts on their return from the midnight service. Miss Stephens had clung gratefully to his arm, as they walked home three abreast, Hetty holding the lantern. He couldn't help contrasting Miss Stephens's fashionably trimmed small hat and warm beaver collar, with the carefully mended costume of his earlier companion.

Several cottagers had passed the window as he picked at his ham that morning, carrying their dinners to the baker's-shop oven. Arthur had appeared promptly after breakfast, clutching two bottles of Madeira and some port to accompany his Stilton. Though he feared the latter may be too strong for the ladies.

Between answering Arthur's genial banter and Miss Stephens's perfect tact, Abbs kept returning to the question foremost on his mind. Who had opened the door between the two houses, if not Jane? And to what purpose? Could it be to throw suspicion on someone from the shop? Chafing at the delay until he could speak to Constable Duffield, he decided he could at least rule out the possibility that Hetty had undrawn the bolt herself.

He escaped to the kitchen, Arthur having commandeered Miss Stephens to help him look over some song-sheets.

'No, there's nothing needs doing. It's good to be together at Christmas, Josiah.'

'It was kind of you to ask me.' Abbs smiled affectionately at her as she stooped before the range. Opening the oven door with a cloth and releasing a blast of hot air.

The kitchen was a cosy place. Smut curled on the corner chair, pretending to doze on his cushion. Coals glowed behind their bars, the shining copper pans stood ready to boil.

'It was decent of Arthur to bring this.' He spoke casually, reading the label on a bottle of Madeira.

'Wasn't it? He and Dora are getting on very well, don't you think?' Hetty glanced cheerfully at him, her face flushed, before returning to her basting. The goose sizzled as she turned the great mound of potatoes, the air laced with sage and onion.

'They seem to be.'

He'd left Arthur leaning on the piano. Miss Stephens, in her best dress, was gazing up at him from the stool. Hanging eagerly on his every word, as he thumbed through Hetty's music.

'I believe Dora's begun to put aside her disappointment over Bob. Who knows what the new year will bring?'

'It was a lot for Arthur to carry. I wonder he didn't use the connecting door in the hall,' said Abbs, ignoring his sister's remark.

'It hasn't been opened since Charley's funeral. There, it's all going as it should be.' Moving over to the larder, Hetty took out a small bowl. 'The truth is, when Arthur moved above the shop, I thought it best to make a division between the business and my home. I couldn't wish for a better step-son. But he always thinks he knows best and he takes an interest in everything. I didn't want him constantly popping in without warning.'

'I do understand.'

'You don't think I'm ungrateful?' Hetty peered at him while her hands set to work mixing mustard.

'Not at all,' said Abbs with feeling.

'I was glad of him on hand at night while his father was ill. But afterwards, I knew I had to re-make my life and the shop was nothing to do with me anymore. I think it was better for Arthur to know I'd only be in there like any customer. I'd always kept up my dressmaking on the side, as you know. I set myself to building up my own small business and I've never wanted for orders. Sewing helped me through those first weeks of mourning.'

'I regret not being able to visit you then.' Abbs stroked the cat's chin, not looking at her.

'Bless you, I know how it is with your work. These things are sent to try us and we must face them with fortitude. I always knew Charley was a lot older.'

He'd been immersed in an investigation at the time. There'd been no possibility of his unsympathetic superintendent granting him leave. Even so, he should have asked.

'So you keep the connecting door locked?'

'Bolted. The key was lost when we came here. What is this about? You mustn't worry about me, you know.'

'I'm sure your brother is only thinking of our safety, Hetty,' said Miss Stephens, shutting the door behind her.

'I can't forget the parcel that was delivered to you. Hetty told me all about it.' Abbs regarded her neutrally. She had invited him to call her by her given name, the previous evening.

'Josiah.' Hetty's voice was reproachful. 'We shouldn't dwell on such things on Christmas Day.'

'It's true, I am thinking of your safety.'

Miss Stephens, who had gone pale, smiled tremulously at him. 'It is reassuring to have a detective looking after us. It's frightening to think someone bears me malice. I'm sure I've done nothing to deserve it.'

'Don't think of it, Dora. It was the work of a warped mind. Mercifully, nothing's happened since, so try to put it behind you.' Throwing her brother an exasperated look, Hetty patted her friend's shoulder.

'I shall endeavour to. Thank you, Hetty. I came to see if you needed any help? It smells delicious in here.'

'It's all going well. No, thank you, my dear. You get back to Arthur and keep him company.'

'If you're sure. I'll leave you both to continue your conversation.'

'You were a long time seeing Jane home, last night,' said Hetty, when they were alone again.

'It was icy underfoot, if you recall.'

'I wish you could find someone, Josiah. A man should remarry.' When he made no answer, she turned round from prodding the pudding and looked at him, gesturing with the fork. 'You haven't met anyone, I suppose?'

He shook his head. 'No one would have me,' he said lightly. 'You mustn't worry either, Hetty. I do very well as I am.'

Dinner had been a lavish affair, with Arthur making a great performance of both carving the goose, then carrying in the flaming pudding. Later, there had been generous slices of Hetty's twelfth-cake and a cold collation for those who could manage it. Abbs could not, though Arthur had heaped his plate and been absently popping sugar-plums in his mouth ever since.

Glancing at the mantle clock, he resigned himself to a last effort, before their guest would surely leave. Miss Stephens yawned delicately behind her hand, graceful as a cat.

'Capital, just the thing as you say, Ma. There's no one like Mr. Dickens to round off Christmas night.'

Hetty leant forward expectantly, her embroidery forgotten at last. Her hands were rarely still when she sat down. 'What about *The Haunted House?*'

Finding the page, Abbs cleared his throat and began to read.

~

On the morning of Boxing Day, Constable Duffield was to be found in uniform, standing in the doorway of the police house and showing out a visitor. Abbs stood aside and raised his hat, as the well-dressed matron stepped into the street. Inclining her head, she looked him up and down, like an undertaker assessing height, before turning away.

'Come away in, Mr. Abbs. D'you mind the office this time?'

'Not at all. Enjoy your day off?'

'Well now, is Christmas Day really all it's cracked up to be? Thing is, my brother-in-law and I aren't over-fond of one another. Generally, our paths don't cross. But all yesterday we were like two sardines in a tin at my sister's place, with all the young 'uns. I'm glad to get back to my desk.'

'You've had an early customer.'

'That was Mrs Merrick, the vicar's lady.' He gave Abbs an expressive look that conveyed his opinion. 'Not police business at all. She has a bee in her bonnet about the choir boys. Reckons she and the vicar found a bag of gobstoppers in the vestry. It's my belief they were his and he didn't dare tell her. Did you enjoy the music, sir?'

'I'm no judge but it seemed to me very fine.'

Duffield looked gratified. 'That's handsome of you, considering Mrs Byers mentioned you live in a cathedral city. I don't suppose you came to discuss the festivities, grateful though I was to be invited to Mrs Byers' house.'

Declining the offer of tea, Abbs gave him an edited version of his conversation with Jane Goddard. 'You were quite right to be reticent,' he concluded. 'The young woman is mortified and would be more so, if she realised you know everything. Better to be warned off by a stranger she'll never see again.'

Sitting at his desk, Duffield studied him. 'You'll be back sometime to stay with Mrs Byers, though?'

Abbs realised he did not expect to return to Aylmer. 'It will be a long time before I can get away again. I don't need to tell you a detective's leave is meagre. This is my yearly allowance.'

'I'm grateful to you, Mr. Abbs. I'm sure young Jane will be in time. She might not realise it yet, while she's grieving, but she's had a narrow escape.

'I believe she's minded to behave herself. She's had a bad shock. She'll be able to think first and govern her temper from now on.'

'Well, you've all but cleared up the crime rate for us.' Duffield reached behind his chair, replacing a ledger on a shelf.

'Not true,' said Abbs. 'Someone left the pig's head for Miss Stephens and I intend to find out who.'

'I understand you're leaving us soon. How d'you intend to go about it, might I ask?'

'Would you be willing to do some checking for me? I've no right to take up your time but you can ask questions I can't here.'

Duffield leant forward with interest. 'After the favour you've done me? Gladly. Tell me what you need and I'll get on to it straight away.'

'Could you talk to the butcher's again in the nearest village, Reddenham, is it?'

'That's right, three mile away. They supply Aylmer since our chap gave up. No one wanted to take it on as a meat-shop. It'd been run down for a time and by then Hope's in Reddenham had all the trade.'

'I know they deliver but I want you to ask if a particular person ever calls in. It might jog someone's memory. You still have the date when the parcel was left, I take it?'

'All in here.' The constable tapped his regulation notebook lying on the desk.

'Good.'

Duffield's eyebrows rose as Abbs outlined the questions to ask. 'Begging your pardon, Mr. Abbs, are you sure about this?'

'I believe so, though proving it's another matter. That's why I need any confirmation to be found.' Picking up his hat, Abbs stood. 'My thanks. I'll bid you good morning, Constable. My sister and I have been invited to sit with Mrs Tillson this afternoon. I'm hoping to learn something more from her.'

'Call in when you get back, Mr. Abbs and I'll have what you need.'

~

He'd spent the forenoon reading the *Norfolk News* and listening to Hetty reminisce as she sewed by the fire. Miss Stephens had excused herself, explaining she needed to work on the costume for the vicar's wife, which was on the dressmaker's model.

'That woman's impossible,' said Hetty, rummaging in her Tunbridge box. 'Her gown's almost finished and she decided she wants an elaborate trim on the over-skirt. It isn't the cost, it's the extra work. She won't allow us any more time.'

'She'd been brow-beating Constable Duffield earlier.'

Hetty gave him a searching glance as she produced a lump of beeswax and stiffened her thread. 'I was saying to Dora that you and Mr. Duffield are seeing a lot of one another. You had your heads together on Christmas Eve. She pointed out you have your work in common and it's only natural you should enjoy talking to him. But I know that look of old, Josiah. I told her, it's my belief you're up to something.'

At that point, they'd heard the thud of the letter-box and Abbs jumped up to fetch her the second post.

The ground was still iron hard as they set out to walk to Mrs Tillson's cottage. A weak sun was attempting to break through a grey sky.

'Do many people take this path through the copse?' said Abbs, as they turned towards the trees.

'If they're going to the farm cottages. It's quicker than taking the lane. That loops round past the station. Villagers come here to collect kindling.'

'You don't mind crossing the track since the accident?'

'I'm not fanciful. I couldn't be more sorry for Bob but life has to go on. If he'd died under carriage wheels, we'd still have to use the road.'

'It must have been a terrible shock for you all, particularly Miss Stephens.'

'Oh, it was.' Hetty shook her head sadly. 'Dora has never spoken of it but she's been subdued since it happened. She was sewing a trousseau in her room in the evenings. I saw by accident once. She was embroidering a silk nightgown. Not that she can't stitch what she likes in front of me. I wouldn't tease her but she has a private nature.'

'When did you hear the news?' Halting, his attention was on dislodging a stone from the sole of his boot. He had heard all the details from Duffield, but that wasn't what he wanted to know.

'Not until the next morning. Constable Duffield came in the shop and told Arthur. He came straight away to tell us.'

Couldn't wait to recount such a momentous piece of news, thought Abbs. It had been dusk when Bob Fuller was killed. The train driver had seen and felt nothing in the failing light, so Duffield had said, which was perfectly possible. It was only when they'd reached the terminus at King's Lynn that a fireman had noticed unmistakable signs on the engine and the police had been informed.

There was no railway detective force in the county, so a search had been organised by the regular constabulary. He could imagine the chain of railwaymen and constables strung out along the track. Duffield had been one of them. It had started to rain, he said, the damp air smelt of brackish Fen water.

They would have tramped along the clinker. Swaying from side to side as they searched the dark, their wavering string of flickering lamps held aloft. Then a shout or a whistle blown, when one of them made the first, grim discovery. There had been several.

'How did Miss Stephens take it?'

'She went as white as a pillowslip. Though, come to think of it, she looked wan at the breakfast table. She'd been indisposed the previous afternoon and had to lie down. Arthur said Jane nearly swooned when she heard. Grace was horrified when they worked out Bob had died after leaving her mother.'

'No one would have missed Mr. Fuller, living alone as he did.'

'No, but in any case, no one could have saved him. It must have happened in an instant and that's the only mercy.'

The train had gone by at its accustomed time. Duffield had assured him the inquest had turned up nothing untoward. In the circumstances, the post-mortem report would have no more to tell.

'And no villager was around to see the accident? You and Miss Stephens were indoors, Arthur, Grace and Jane in the shop, Mrs Tillson inside her cottage. What about her neighbours?'

'Her nearest neighbour, old Bart Swaley, would have been in the Barley Mow by then. Arthur wasn't in the shop. He was out on a delivery but he'd have been nowhere near. The lane's a dead end.' She let her unfortunate phrase fall away.

Abbs let the subject drop. Hetty had already accused him of being like a dog with a bone. They continued in silence. A solitary blackbird flitted from branch to branch just ahead of them. Taking flight when he was startled by the abrupt cough of a pheasant, beyond the trees.

'It is good of you to give up your time like this, Josiah. I know Grace is grateful.'

'Not at all, I like meeting people.'

'We've offered you little in the way of entertainment, I'm afraid.'

'I've been glad of the rest.' Abbs smiled at her, shifting the basket he was carrying. 'And we've had time to talk.'

'Only two more days though. I wondered, would you care to visit Hunstanton tomorrow? We could easily catch the train. It would make a change to have a blow by the sea and I did enjoy being out with you.'

'I'd like nothing better. What ails Mrs Tillson exactly?'

'A weakness of the heart. She isn't bed-ridden but she can't walk far. It's a good job she has Grace to help her.'

They were approaching the railway line, where the dead posy was nowhere to be seen. He hoped Jane would look to a brighter future, as they all must.

For his own part, there was still the question of London to be decided. The work at Great Scotland Yard would undoubtedly hold more interest and get him away from the hostility of his superintendent.

His recent murder enquiry had been successfully solved but at a great cost. That case had made him realise it was time to put aside past mistakes. The metropolis drew men and women from all corners of the Empire. Each one seeking a fresh start, so why not him?

In the course of that case, he had made some new acquaintance who were moving to the capital. He supposed, in such a vast city, it was unlikely he would encounter them again.

He thought of the able young sergeant who'd worked with him. His assistance had been invaluable in solving their investigation.

Sergeant Reeve was London born. At their last meeting, he'd expressed his dissatisfaction and talked of himself requesting a transfer to the capital, where he still had family. If he asked the Chief Constable, might there be an opening for Reeve at the Yard? Would this be helpful or seen as interference?

'It's this first one,' said Hetty as they neared the farm cottages. This time, Abbs studied them with interest as they approached. Bob Fuller was unlikely to have been seen by any of Mrs Tillson's neighbours when he left. He was sure now that Fuller had been waylaid. Somewhere near the railway crossing, out of sight on the way through the wood.

The nearer cottage, which had 'Albert' incised in the stone over the door, was much neater than its pair. Trim, starched nets hung at the small windows. Dolphin door-knocker and letter-box gleamed, the step had been whitened. Presumably it was all cared for by Grace, stooping with her stiff hip in the few hours left between serving at the grocer's.

Small wonder she liked to disappear in a novel, thought Abbs, as he eyed the grimy windows of 'Victoria.' From behind the second pair of cottages, came the unmistakable whiff of pig.

Rapping on the door, Hetty opened it at once, calling cheerfully. 'It's only me, Maggie, and I've brought my brother.'

Beckoned to follow, Abbs entered a parlour made smaller by a dark, leafy paper, and heavy furniture against the walls. Introductions were made and he decided, when they were settled by the fire, that the bureau, sideboard and looking-glass were survivors from a larger house.

'I see you're admiring my sideboard, Mr. Abbs.' Mrs Tillson looked at him expectantly.

'I was, ma'am. It's a handsome piece of furniture.'

He had been looking for somewhere to set down his tea cup, the small table being crowded. Politeness had required him to accept a large scone, which looked remarkably like Mrs Tillson's footstool. The fire was suffocating and a button on the back of the chair kept jabbing his spine.

'Indian rosewood. I've some lovely things and it cheers me to look at them. I was in service before I married, to a doctor's widow, such a kind lady. When she was going to live with her son and his family and I was to be wed, she told me to pick three items. "Fanny won't care for them and I know you will, Margaret," she said to me. That was her daughter by marriage.'

Attending dutifully, Abbs was reaching for a reply when Hetty stepped in.

'Grace polishes them beautifully.'

'I couldn't wish for a better daughter but I'd be glad to see her safely settled. She's a wonderful housekeeper, Mr. Abbs and in the end, that's what counts. A fair face won't last but a light hand with pastry will.' Dabbing a napkin on her upper chin, Mrs Tillson fixed her gaze on him.

Feeling like a worm spotted by a bright-eyed robin, Abbs glared at Hetty. Her mouth was twitching. He forgave her when their hostess spoke again.

'As a matter of fact, I thought our troubles were come to an end this year. There was a time when I reckoned something in the wind between Grace and Bob.' She turned to Hetty, her manner confidential.

'That can't be right, Maggie?' Watching them both, Abbs saw his sister look perplexed.

'I know, dear, better than anyone. You can understand my thinking it at first, when he paid me such attention. Getting round the mother to clear the path to the daughter, I thought. As it turned out, I couldn't have been more mistaken. Hetty will have spoken to you about the neighbour we lost, Mr. Abbs? A horrid accident. And me, the last earthly soul who spoke to him. Do help yourself to another, I can see you like them.'

'Thank you,' said Abbs. 'Hetty did tell me about Mr. Fuller's tragic death. I believe you and your daughter lost a firm friend?'

'I can see you're a sympathetic person. Grace said you spoke very nicely to her. Yes, Mr. Fuller was a general favourite. He was the druggist, you see. That's how we met. Grace became acquainted with him first. He brought my medicine one day and we got on famously. After that, he'd often drop in at tea-time. Sometimes he'd walk Grace home from the shop. He'd tell me who he'd seen that day. Sometimes he'd read me the court circular, with what the Prince of Wales was doing and all the royal children.'

He had noticed the collection of commemorative china. A plate marking the death of the Prince Consort stood on the bureau. 'Mr. Fuller had settled happily in Aylmer, then?'

'Oh, he had. That's why it was such a particular tragedy. He came here with such high hopes, you see. "This is the very place for me, Mrs T," he used to say. Sitting in that chair you're in now, Mr. Abbs. "It was a lucky chance for me when I saw my premises advertised, just at the right time. Here I am and here I mean to stay."' Sitting back in her chair, Mrs Tillson's eyes glistened. 'Be a pal, Hetty and do the honours. Top up the pot for me.'

Taking the teapot and rescuing Abbs from his plate, Hetty went into the other room. Mrs Tillson rallied, smiling kindly at him.

Expecting someone frail, he had been surprised to meet a lady of extremely stout proportions and a high colour. Mrs Tillson seemed to suffer with dropsy, which had, he thought, some connection with a weak heart. She bore no resemblance to her daughter.

'Between these walls, Bob confided in me, Mr. Abbs, only a week or so before he died. He was all excited and wanted to tell someone. He asked me to keep it to myself, which I did faithfully, but it can't hurt now.'

He smiled encouragingly at her. 'It may help you to speak of it, Mrs Tillson.'

'You're a good listener, like Hetty. I believe it would. It doesn't do to keep things bottled up. I haven't even said a word to Grace. The pity of it is, that Bob had just had a letter from his betrothed. Yes, you may well look surprised. None of us knew there was any such person. They'd been making arrangements. She wrote to him that it was all settled for the banns to take place. He was about to bring her to Aylmer as his bride.'

'But Maggie, how can that possibly be right? He was courting Dora.' Hetty stood in the open doorway, holding the teapot in both hands.

Behind her, Abbs could see a worn step down to the scullery and a bacon hook, hanging from a broad beam. He drew further back as she brushed past him, skirts rustling, her eyes intent on Mrs Tillson's face.

'He never was, he said as much to me.' Mrs Tillson paused as Hetty refilled their cups. 'Thank you, dear. Oh, I know there was gossip in the beginning. I think Bob felt awkward about it, not wanting to give Miss Stephens a false impression. He accompanied her to a musical evening, when he first came here, but there was a misunderstanding. He was under the impression they'd be in a party with your Arthur and some others. He wouldn't have hurt a fly on purpose. People like that can't always say what they mean.'

'You won't say any of this to anyone else, not even Grace?' Hetty put her hand on her friend's sleeve. 'I shouldn't like to see Dora hurt.'

'I shan't tell a soul. It's a comfort to have shared it with you both. As for Grace, she feels badly enough that Bob died on his way home from visiting me. It would add to her sadness to think there's a young woman left bereaved.'

'Why didn't he tell any of us he was betrothed?'

'Some people are private by nature,' said Abbs. 'You said that yourself on the way here, Hetty. Because they're affable, it doesn't follow they reveal everything about themselves.'

'Mr. Abbs is right. None of us were friends of long-standing, after all. Some folk don't speak of their plans before they're all cut and dried. It never does to tempt fate.'

'Well, I think he behaved foolishly,' said Hetty. She sat stiff-backed, wearing a stubborn look Abbs recalled from his childhood. 'He'd no business to come among us as though he were a free man. No business at all. It was false pretences. It caused a lot of upset.'

'I did wonder how Bob's sweetheart would learn of his death,' said Mrs Tillson. 'It occurred to me I ought to speak to Constable Duffield. But then I heard a friend of Bob's was coming to take away his effects. He told me his young lady was the sister of his oldest friend, you see.'

'The constable found the friend's name and address among Mr. Fuller's papers, I believe.' Abbs rubbed his brow absently, as he spoke. 'Duffield was told nothing of this. But why should he be? It was a matter of private grief.'

'Who was this young woman, Maggie?'

'Her name was Elizabeth, that I do recall. Lizzie, Bob called her. He showed me her likeness in his pocket-book. She had a fetching face. He said she was in service as a nursery-maid, until he could get established and save enough to send for her. There's no truer text than *"In the midst of life, we are in death."* We never know what's round the corner.'

'Very true,' said Abbs.

'I shall never understand what Bob was doing that evening he died.' Mrs Tillson gazed at the likeness on the mantel shelf, as though seeking answers from her own lost husband.

'What do you mean, Mrs Tillson?' He leant forward. She turned to him in surprise at his urgent tone.

'Why was poor Bob knocked down by the London train, Mr. Abbs? He left here a good five and twenty minutes before it comes through. I could set my clock by it.'

Three

Constable Duffield had done all that was requested of him. It was not his fault they were no further forward. Abbs listened as Duffield told him that no one at the butchers' could recall his suspect purchasing a pig's head.

'It was a faint hope, I suppose. So I still haven't a shred of proof.'

'Doesn't mean you're wrong, Mr. Abbs. It's a pity you can't get confirmation but even if you're right, it wasn't a crime. I can see why you're worried about Mrs Byers, of course.'

Abbs made up his mind. He had been weighing up whether to tell Duffield what he really believed. Sighing, he moved away from leaning against the dresser and pulled out a kitchen chair.

'Perhaps I will have that drink after all, if I may. I'm awash with tea.'

'I'd be interested in your opinion and I'm as off-duty as I'm likely to be, barring accidents.' Duffield wiped a glass and filled it from a firkin in the corner. He was holding it up to the window, studying the cloudy liquid, when Abbs spoke again.

'The trouble is, Constable, I think a serious crime *has* been committed. I believe Robert Fuller's death was not due to an accident.'

There was silence. Duffield set down the glass before him with exaggerated care. 'D'you mean he was murdered, sir?'

Abbs shook his head. 'Not murder. I think he was assaulted and that led to his death.'

The afternoon relinquished the last of its light. Their glasses of cider stood forgotten as he outlined his supposition. Duffield listened intently.

When he finished, Abbs waited while the constable stood, his chair legs scraping against the floor. He drained half his glass and moved to the window, looking out at the dusk.

'Say something.'

'It's plausible, Mr. Abbs. But who's to say you're right? Seems to me, you could make out an equal case for two of them. We'd have to check who was in the shop.'

'That's true but alibis can be broken. I've told you who my money's on.'

'You're off in three days?'

Abbs nodded. 'I cannot delay, I'm expected back on duty.'

'I'm sorry, Mr. Abbs. I'm jiggered if I can see how to prove it either way.' Turning up his lamp, Duffield carried it to the table. The flame wavered and a warm, oily smell insinuated around the room. 'I'll do all I can to watch over Mrs Byers for you.'

'Thank you. I appreciate your saying that, but it may not be enough.'

A constrained air had settled between them. Almost, thought Abbs, as though a third party were present. He had played no part in easing Hetty's loss. He would not, could not risk her safety.

'We need a confession.' Duffield had resumed his seat and was tapping his glass.

Abbs smiled faintly at him. 'I doubt we'll get one. There may be another way. A doubtful strategy but it's all I can think of.'

'Go on, sir.'

'I grew up on a shooting estate. This time of year, when I was a boy, I'd occasionally earn a little pocket money as a beater. Didn't really have the stomach for it. I felt sorry for the birds but it was expected. It would have come back on my father if I'd refused. Anyway, I soon found that if you blunder about clumsily and make enough noise, the birds will break cover. You'll set them running. In a sense, that's what I mean to do. See if I can put up a bird.'

~

'I thought I'd look in this evening and see Josiah, as he's leaving us soon. He's still looking peaky, don't you agree, Ma?'

Hetty studied him solicitously. 'You do still look tired, you know.'

'Nonsense, I feel fine.' Picking up the cards Arthur had dealt him, Abbs endeavoured to turn his mind to the game. He hadn't intended to be short with Hetty. She wasn't the one irritating him. Looking up, he found Miss Stephens, seated opposite, was regarding him with concern.

'You must have a great deal to occupy your thoughts. Perhaps your mind is already back at your desk?'

'I think you've hit on it, Miss Dora. I saw you coming out of the police-house earlier, Josiah. Never off duty, eh? You ought to take up a hobby, man.'

'I suppose being a detective does give me an instinct for wrong-doing,' said Abbs, laying down a card.

'Hear that? We must watch ourselves. I've nothing to hide.' Arthur chuckled, 'I'm sure I've never given short measure.'

'Arthur, as if Josiah would even think such a thing. Stop teasing. Spades are trumps, you said?' Hetty pushed her spectacles higher on the bridge of her nose

'Be careful, Hetty, I can see your hand,' said Miss Stephens.

'Whereas Josiah holds his close to his chest, eh?' Arthur turned up a corner of the top card before claiming it. 'Capital, just what I need.'

'I wonder who among us holds the ace? Abbs looked at the others in turn. 'Isn't that known as the death card?'

'Let's not be morbid.' Hetty lay down a card and picked up another.

Miss Stephens flicked a glance at Abbs. Their eyes met and she returned to her hand.

'Mind you, we do have a mystery to solve,' said Arthur. 'We never did get to the bottom of the Aylmer joker. Now you mustn't worry, Miss Dora. You're quite safe here with us to protect you.'

'You're too good.'

'We heard another mystery this afternoon,' said Abbs carelessly.

'Well? Don't keep it to yourself.' Arthur looked eagerly at him.

'It was nothing. Only some silly gossip from Maggie Tillson.' Hetty glared at Abbs. 'I think I'll put some more coal on.'

Miss Stephens shivered delicately, drawing her shawl closer to her neck. 'It certainly is a cold night. I predict snow before the year's out.'

'I'll see to it in a minute,' said Arthur. 'Let's hear Josiah's mystery.'

Undeterred by Hetty looking daggers at him, Abbs repeated what Mrs Tillson had told them about the time Bob Fuller had left her.

'Maggie spends every afternoon with her head buried in scandal-sheets and novels. That's why she was keen to meet a real detective. She has too much time on her hands and imagines mysteries where there are none.' Rising abruptly from the table, Hetty took out her vexation with the poker.

'It's an odd story all the same. Fuller had been here long enough to know the train times.' Arthur stroked his whiskers, his cards face down on the table. 'There must be a simple explanation. Could have been caught, er, taken ill.' He nodded significantly, jerking his head towards the ladies. 'Least said, soonest mended.'

Not for Bob Fuller, thought Abbs. He was not displeased with his evening's work.

~

Abbs was quietly amused that Hetty spent much of their train journey to Hunstanton, scolding him for his lack of tact on the previous evening. Miss Stephens had pleaded a headache and retired early. Arthur, clearly disappointed to lose her presence, had still lingered late.

He was not, he confided in Abbs, over-fond of his own company. The winter evenings hung heavily in his rooms behind the shop. What's more, there was no sense in two fires, when they could be sitting together.

'I've said my piece. Now let's enjoy the day. Dora's working hard at home and I feel as though I'm playing truant.'

Despite nearing her fiftieth year, she still had the artless manner of a school-girl, thought Abbs fondly. Hetty's temper never lasted. She had a capacity for enjoying herself that many women lost, or life mislaid for them.

They had the compartment to themselves at that time of year. In summer, it would have been a packed excursion train, she assured him, while fixing her hat-pin more firmly.

'You came to bed late,' he said, watching her stifle a yawn.

'I was finishing off Mrs Merrick's gown. Dora's a first class seamstress but I felt I should see to it myself, the wretched woman insisted. I hope I didn't disturb you.'

'I was reading. Couldn't get off.' Sleep had eluded him again and he'd gone over every nuance of the days he'd spent in Aylmer. Working out when he'd first felt something was wrong. Recalling looks and scraps of conversation.

'The sea air will do me good. You are well wrapped up, Josiah?'

'Don't you start. Arthur treats me as though I'm his venerable uncle and I'm what... six or seven years his elder?'

'Seven. It's only his way. Do look...' Hetty broke off, pointing at the window. 'There's the sea. We're here at last.'

Handing her down, Abbs looked around at the station which had been built, like so many, in the last decade. They were on a long island platform with the sea directly in front of them. In summer, Hunstanton would be an appealing place. At the end of the year, the grey, German Ocean looked cold and indifferent.

They made their way past a good many shops, where the Christmas decorations were looking tawdry long before Twelfth Night. Then they wandered among pleasant streets and squares of smart houses, their trees just sufficiently mature to be losing that raw look of new building.

Hetty was perfectly happy strolling along, her arm tucked into his, exclaiming at everything. Abbs was glad they had escaped the oppressive atmosphere of Aylmer. He knew he had no choice other than to leave Norfolk the day after next.

'Do let's go along the pier. Don't you think it looks fine?'

'By all means. Yes, I wouldn't have known the place.'

'The land-owner invested a fortune, so they say. He brought the railway and had whole streets put up. Now his son reaps all his foresight.'

'His rents and railway-shares must be worth a pretty penny.'

They were standing on a slight elevation called The Green. Hetty had expressed a wish to walk as far as the lighthouse, situated on the edge of the low cliffs. The view encompassed the carrstone buildings of the growing town, the open sea and the estuary of The Wash.

On a clear day, they could have seen twenty miles or so across to the neighbouring county of Lincolnshire, but that coast was blurred in cloud.

Looking inland, Abbs idly watched another train drawn up in the sidings by the gasworks. Workmen were shovelling its load of coal. A number of seaside resorts seemed to be the vision of a single man, he reflected.

He supposed they were a sound business venture, the southern equivalent of owning a mine or a mill, even. New Hunstanton was unrecognisable from the fishing village he had visited as a boy.

The estate servants had been on their summer outing and Hetty had been helping to organise games for the children. A few cottages sold teas and it had been his first time in a boat. He had rarely cause to venture in one since. Would he still be sick if he did?

The idea of a planned town rolled out to order, with the strings held by one man, didn't appeal to him. He was drawn to old streets where haphazard buildings leaned against one another, marking the passage of centuries.

In London, they were tearing down old parts by the week. It was said in the 'papers that whole neighbourhoods could rise up in three months. And the dust-heaps, for such a vast population, were as high as eaves.

They were to eat at the big hotel across The Green. That had been there years ago, the first building of the planned expansion. Now, the name had changed and it no longer stood on its own. Things never really stood still. You just wished they would.

He was middle-aged in outlook, finding the pace of modern life too swift. Whereas Hetty, several yards ahead with one hand on the brim of her hat, was laughing and beckoning him on. He hurried to catch up with her.

A few hardy folk were ambling on the pier like themselves. An elderly gentleman, seated on one of the benches, raised his hat and wished them good day.

'When was this opened?'

'It must be three summers ago.'

They leant on the railings, looking back at the curious striped cliffs with their three bands of yellowy-brown carrstone, red sandstone and white chalk. Abbs knew that their geological rarity brought many scientific gentlemen to view them and search for fossils.

'The sea air's given me quite an appetite, Josiah. Are you ready for some refreshment?'

~

Afterwards, they both agreed that the day had been an enjoyable interlude. After happily looking over her purchases, Hetty had fallen asleep on the return journey. The weather had become inclement by mid-afternoon, with a yellowy tinge to the low, grey sky. Together with the barometer rising slightly that morning, it indicated snow.

The lamps were lit in the grocer's as they passed. Jane was arranging the window display, as she had been on his first morning. The difference was that she looked up and smiled at them both. Abbs was pleased she showed no trace of embarrassment at seeing him.

'I've enjoyed today so much,' said Hetty, opening the door. 'Why is it though, that a day out is always more fatiguing than a day spent in work? You go and see Dora and get warm. I'll put the kettle on directly.' Swiftly removing her outer garments, leaving her gloves and parcels on the hall table, she swept through to the scullery.

The house was silent, the door to the sewing-room shut tight. Abbs went to the foot of the stairs and listened. He felt sure they were the only ones there. Glancing round the dining-room door, he joined Hetty in the kitchen.

'No sign of Dora? She must be out. She often likes to get a breath of fresh air after sitting indoors all day. Or she may be lying down.' Hetty looked at the ceiling and lowered her voice. 'I'm concerned about her. She hasn't seemed quite well for a while. Constant headaches and that could be her eyes. We do so much close work. I wonder if I should suggest she sees an oculist? What's that?'

Straightening up, Abbs handed her a tiny button he had spotted, among the folds of the rag rug, by the hearth.

Hetty turned it over in her palm. 'That's from my button box. How did that get in here?' Shrugging, she slipped it in her pocket. 'Shall we go through? I'll bring the tray in a minute. I ought to see if Dora's in her room.'

Abbs paused on the hall runner, as something crunched beneath his boot. Lifting his foot, he saw a thin shard of blue glass, speckled with silver paint. A spot of blood appeared on his finger as he touched it. 'It's from a Christmas ornament.'

Hetty made a vexed sound. 'Smut's tried to run up the tree again. He'll have the whole thing over before we're done.' She threw open the parlour door and came to a standstill on the threshold.

The Christmas tree was indeed over. Upended from its pot, it lay with its top almost reaching the cold grate. The fire, Hetty had laid early that morning, had not been lit. Abbs viewed the scene from over her shoulder.

She stepped into the room and they surveyed the damage. Pine needles were scattered over the carpet, their scent mingling unpleasantly with Arthur's stale cigar smoke. The glass baubles were smashed, not one remained intact. Candles were dislodged, sweets everywhere, only the plaid bows were still tied to the stiff branches thrust in the air.

'What in the world's happened here?'

'Well I don't think you can blame that on the cat,' said Abbs grimly.

He was looking at what had been the bisque angel crowning the tree. The figure lay face upwards, except there was no longer a face. It had been stamped on and ground to powder beneath a heel. A frame had been flung down nearby, the glass cracked. He felt no surprise to recognise his own likeness.

'I don't understand, have we been burgled? Who would do such a thing? Where's Dora?' Hetty stared at him, swallowing.

Abbs didn't answer. He simply looked at her with great weariness and watched the comprehension wash over her face.

She clapped her hand to her mouth. 'Surely... no, that can't be. Why would she..?' Her voice died away. 'I'll check upstairs.'

He listened to the sound of her hurried feet, a door being flung open, silence. Then more doors and the sound of her climbing to the attic. As he was righting the tree, Hetty hurried back, out of breath.

'Dora's room's empty and her things, they're all gone. Everything's bare. It's as if she was never here.'

Amen to that, thought Abbs. 'I'm sorry, Hetty.'

'Tell me what's going on, Josiah? I'm not a complete fool, even if I've been taken for one. I can tell you know what's behind this. You were acting very oddly last night. Did you know Dora was leaving today? Is that why you took me out of the way?' Hetty stood, biting her lip, a hand clasping the chain on her bodice, winding it round her fingers.

'I'll tell you everything I know,' said Abbs gently. 'Which isn't much, actually. No, I didn't know she was going to do this. Do you think I'd have gone out and let her? There was no question of getting you out of the way. The trip was your idea, remember? I was pleased to have a day together, away from this place.'

Hetty nodded abruptly. 'I don't know what's come over me. Of course you didn't foresee this. But you know more than I do. Why should Dora go without telling me and why in the world ruin the tree?' She gestured helplessly at the wreckage before them. A sudden thought struck her. 'You got on well with Dora when you first came but as the days have gone by, you've changed. You've been polite but distant. Has something passed between you?'

'Heaven forbid. Let's leave this mess for now. Come and sit down in the dining-room. I'd like to get Constable Duffield here too.'

'No, Josiah. Angry as I am, I don't want to report her. What's the point? We can keep this to ourselves.'

'It isn't that. I've been speaking to Duffield about Miss Stephens. He should hear what's happened.'

Hetty allowed Abbs to usher her into the hall, closing the door behind them.

'Wait. The button in the kitchen, my box...'

'I'll look,' said Abbs instantly. Opening the door to the sewing-room, he saw and looked back at Hetty. He couldn't shield her.

With a sharp intake of breath, she came slowly into the room, her face white.

'Careful where you step. There are pins everywhere.'

'How could she? Dora must have hated me.' Hetty turned to him, her expression bewildered. 'All that work ruined. Why would she do that to me?'

The day-dress for Mrs Merrick was finished on the dressmaker's model. Skilfully cut by Hetty, after studying a Paris fashion plate, the maroon silk was divided and gathered with elaborate ruffles into a soft tournure, revealing a contrasting rose underskirt. The front of the dress was slashed and torn as though the wearer had been repeatedly stabbed.

Hetty's collection of buttons spilled across the carpet. Her workbox had been ransacked and a basket of trims, lengths of lace and flounces were thrown in a tangle.

'I treated her like a daughter..' Hetty flinched as the door-knocker was given a quick double rap, followed immediately by the sound of the front door being opened.

They hastened back into the hall, Abbs pulling the door closed behind him, as Arthur appeared.

'I saw you both go by but I was busy serving. Thought you'd like to know, Ma, Miss Dora got off all right. I must say,' Arthur wagged his finger at them. 'I'd have thought you'd forego your day out but she said she'd begged you not to. What with you being off soon yourself, Josiah. Most unselfish of her. We shall miss her company but she hopes to be back among us before too long. She was very grateful for my assistance.'

'I'm sure she was,' said Abbs, planting himself before the sewing-room door. He gave Hetty an almost imperceptible shake of his head, as she looked at him.

'What exactly did Dora tell you?' Her voice sounded cracked and she moistened her lips.

'Why, that she'd received a letter from a distant relative, an elderly lady who was seriously ill and needed nursing. She had to go to her at once. A cousin, I think she said. She was most agitated. We thought she was completely alone, didn't we? I did wonder..' Arthur hesitated and touched his moustache, 'if she has expectations. Shall we have tea and you can tell me all about it, Ma?'

'Unfortunately, Hetty's on her way upstairs to lie down,' said Abbs. 'She's come back with a dreadful headache and I fear the onset of a bilious attack.'

'You sat with your back to the engine, I'll be bound. You look awfully pale.'

Hetty smiled faintly. 'I think you're right, Arthur. If you'll excuse me.'

'Of course. Josiah will see you have all you need? Capital. I'll look in tomorrow, then.'

'I'll see you out.' Abbs detached himself from the door. 'Where did Miss Stephens say she was bound for? She did tell us where her relative lives, of course, but everything was rushed at breakfast. She had to go and pack at once and she forgot to leave a direction.'

'Manchester. Quite a journey for a young, unaccompanied woman. I advised her to put up at the station hotel at Euston and continue in the morning.'

'Did she ask you to take her to the station?'

Shutting the gate and leaning on it, Arthur looked affronted. 'Certainly not. She came in the shop to say goodbye to me and naturally, I offered to assist her. She couldn't be expected to manage her trunk by herself. Did she tell Ma how long she expects to be away?'

'I believe not. Who can say in matters of illness? What train did Miss Stephens catch?'

'The 10.50. That's the London express.'

They had left for their own train before nine. 'It's fortunate Miss Stephens had sufficient ready money for her journey,' said Abbs. He wondered if Hetty kept much cash in the house.

Arthur looked shifty of a sudden and fiddled with the turned down tip of his collar. 'As a matter of fact, she wasn't sure she did. The poor girl was terribly embarrassed. It was to be our secret. She was mortified, hadn't liked to ask Ma for an advance. I told her she was a foolish little thing. We're all friends here.' He coughed, self-consciously. 'She's going to write to me directly she's had a chance to go to the bank. We shall correspond while she's away.'

'I'm sure Miss Stephens was deeply grateful she found a good Samaritan,' said Abbs. 'I'd better get back to Hetty.'

'And I'd best go and cash up. You know, Josiah, I'm sorry for this sick, old lady, but it's an ill wind. This has brought things on famously between Dora and me.'

Abbs watched him disappear in the grocer's before going in. Hetty was in the parlour, hands on hips, surveying the damage.

'That's got rid of him for the night at least. Well done, Hetty.'

'I couldn't cope with all the repercussions. Arthur will chew over this for months if we tell him, endlessly discussing why she did it.'

'I agree, it's better he never knows. Particularly as he drove Miss Stephens to the station and lent her enough money to get to Manchester.'

'Manchester? Dora told me she was living in Norwich when she replied to my advertisement.'

Abbs shrugged. 'Who knows if that woman ever spoke a true word? She probably mentioned somewhere at random. It's more original than London. We're unlikely to hear more of her.'

'I need to hear everything you know, Josiah.' Hetty looked at him sternly. 'Dora Stephens lived under my roof for months and I thought we were the best of friends. She could have made her home with me always. I can see I've been extremely foolish with my trust but I've a right to know what brought this on.'

'Of course you do. Let me get Constable Duffield, if he's there, and I'll explain what I think happened. Please, Hetty, go and sit in the dining-room or the kitchen. You've had a bad shock. You've still some brandy, haven't you?'

'I don't need a brandy or a sit-down. Nor a smelling-bottle. It has been a shock but I'll weather it. What I need right now is a broom.'

~

'I'm glad to see you, Mr. Abbs. I was going to take the liberty of stepping round after supper.' Constable Duffield, filling his doorway, paused to raise a hand to a passer-by in the street. He nodded agreeably at his visitor, his eyes lively. 'I've some news I believe will interest you mightily. Come on in. I'll just light the lamp and be with you.'

'I've some news for you,' said Abbs. 'Miss Stephens has fled. Will you come and speak to my sister with me?'

The affability vanished from Duffield's countenance, replaced by a look of keen interest. 'So you were right, sir. The bird has flown. How's Mrs Byers taking it?'

'Very well, considering it's come out of nowhere as far as she's concerned. Stephens packed and left in a hurry, while we were out for the day, but found time to leave a couple of mementos. The Christmas tree was wrecked, all the ornaments smashed.'

Duffield grimaced. 'That's right nasty. No call for that.'

'There's worse. She threw everything around in Hetty's sewing-room and slashed a dress on order for your Mrs Merrick. Hetty will have to make some excuse and that will harm her reputation. You did say the vicar's wife isn't noted for her forbearance.'

'That's downright malicious. After Mrs Byers has been so good to her. Taking her in, giving her work and a decent home. Does she want to bring charges?'

Abbs shook his head dismissively. 'There's no point. Stephens will take good care never to be found. I should like to see Robert Fuller get justice but there's no proof in existence.' He sighed bitterly. 'At least we've driven her out of my sister's home. I'll wait outside for you.'

Duffield went in, reappearing at once to light the lamp, then going back in briefly. Abbs paced on the short path, watching the dark seep like spilt ink across a blotter. Aylmer was becoming a place of shadows. He felt unpleasantly aware of the empty miles of Fens, stretching beyond that side of the village.

Always glad of fresh air and open spaces, he was surprised to find himself missing illuminated streets and the bustle of more people. Perhaps he had left behind the countryside without realising. When Duffield joined him he was carefully carrying something shielded in newspaper, which he held on his side away from Abbs.

Hetty met them at the door, her face convulsed with worry. 'Josiah... Good evening Mr. Duffield.'

'Evening, Mrs Byers. Mr. Abbs told me what's happened. I'm sorry for your troubles.' Duffield removed his hat and thrust forward what he was carrying. Abbs could see now he held a few stems of pale flowers. 'These are for you, ma'am.'

'For me? Christmas roses. They're lovely, thank you.' Raising her head, Abbs saw the glint of threatened tears in his sister's eyes. He moved unobtrusively between them.

'What were you going to say, Hetty?'

'We haven't seen Smut. You don't think..?'

An icy shard twisted in Abbs's guts. 'He's usually out all day, isn't he?' His voice was casual.

'Why don't I have a look around out the back?' said Duffield easily. 'I know your cat by sight, Mrs Byers. 'He's the big fellow. He's probably off hunting.'

'I'll find you some light.' Abbs gestured with a jerk of his head towards the scullery. 'That's good of you.' When they were alone, he opened the back door. 'I hope to God nothing's happened to him. That would finish Hetty. You know, I think Stephens is capable of it.'

'Chances are the cat was safely out of the way. I'll check the out-houses and go a way down the rear path. He might be on his way back for his supper. Have you checked all the house, Mr. Abbs? If there are any more nasty surprises, you don't want Mrs Byers finding them.'

'She glanced round upstairs when we first came in but you're right. I'll do it now.'

Dreading what he might find, Abbs searched the house, entering Hetty's bedroom without compunction and going so far as to turn back the eiderdown. Despite disliking platitudes, he'd heard himself murmuring 'try not to worry' as he passed her.

Miss Stephens's room was bare of personality. All the drawers were hanging open, as if a thief had been at work. The cupboard doors were flung wide, revealing only the empty pegs and a lavender bag. Not so much as a stray hairpin or a speck of powder until he threw back her bedclothes. The sheet and blankets were rumpled, the top pillow still bearing the imprint of her head.

When he returned downstairs after searching the attics, Hetty was clearing up in the parlour. She'd swept the pine needles and decorations into a pile. The broken glass was on newspaper.

'Can I do that for you?'

She shook her head, smoothing a loop of hair that had worked loose behind her ear. 'I'd rather keep busy. See if you can find Mr. Duffield and I'll make some tea.'

'Let me at least take that.' Wrapping the paper round the glass, Abbs went outside. It was fully dark and the oil lamp in the scullery window only shone on a few feet of the garden. Making his way down the path, he went through the back gate and heard Duffield moving about. He was coming along the foot-path, his shadow growing enormous in the light cast by his lantern.

'Any sign?'

'Nothing. I've tried calling. You didn't find anything, Mr. Abbs?'

'Thankfully, no.'

'No news is good news then. Only to my mind, if she'd killed the cat, he'd be in plain sight, not chucked in the woods. I had a careful look round the coal-shed and the wash-house and in the little arbour.'

'Hetty and I are very grateful to you. The flowers were a kind thought.'

It was too dark to read Duffield's expression as he looked up at the sky. 'It's going to snow.'

Hetty was carrying the laden tea-tray as they entered. She swung round, reading their faces. 'I've put a match to the dining-room fire. I'm afraid it'll be a while before it throws out much heat, Mr. Duffield. Thank you for going out into the cold.'

'Think nothing of it, Mrs Byers and don't you fret.' Shaking her head at Abbs's attempt to take the tray from her, Hetty led the way, her head held high. Abbs drew Duffield aside to show him the parlour and sewing-room.

When they were seated at the table, no one spoke. Hetty turned a teaspoon between her fingers, her tea untouched.

'Go on, Josiah. Everything.'

Abbs rubbed his brow while he assembled his thoughts. 'I'm trying to work out when I first felt something was wrong. I suppose it was on the evening I arrived. We were travelling from the station and you told me there'd been some odd goings on in the village. The next day, Arthur described them to me.'

Hetty frowned. 'What does that have to do with Dora smashing my things and leaving without a word?'

'Bear with me and I'll try to explain. Much of this is guesswork or was until now.' He and Duffield exchanged glances. 'Constable Duffield has discovered who was behind those incidents and the matter's been dealt with, didn't you say?'

'That's correct. We won't be troubled by any more pranks, Mrs Byers. No real harm was intended. It was an unhappy soul getting up to mischief. You'll understand I can't say more.'

Nodding doubtfully, Hetty looked from one to the other. 'If you say so, Mr. Duffield. But where does Dora come in? Why was she sent that hateful parcel?'

'That's what I kept wondering,' said Abbs. 'It didn't seem to fit with the other things. Lobbing something at a gatepost and tossing a hat in a pond, for instance, were spur of the moment actions.' He was glad Hetty didn't know about Jane entering Fuller's house, in a moment of madness. 'Going to the trouble of wrapping up a pig's head to look like a present was premeditated and deeply unpleasant. It seemed to me that two people were at work.'

'I ought to have spotted that, myself,' said Duffield.

'No, no, the onlooker sees more of the game. I gave it a lot of thought. Partly, because I was unused to being idle and I like a puzzle. But mostly because it came to your door, Hetty. So I introduced myself to Constable Duffield and he told me something really puzzling.' Abbs indicated that he should take up the tale.

'Fact is, Mrs Byers, when I looked into it, I had a word with your neighbours. I don't know if you recall that Henry opposite, was working out front when you and Miss Stephens left that day?'

Hetty nodded. 'That's right. He had his gate off its hinges.'

'He was there the whole time you were gone and he was certain that no one came to this house. I didn't pass it on for there was no sense in worrying you. I'd hit a blind alley.'

Stirring her tea at last, Hetty took a mouthful. 'That doesn't make sense. Henry must have been mistaken.'

'He was sure not, ma'am.'

'In that case,' said Abbs, 'the only other possibility was that someone had entered this house and pushed the parcel out through the front door, taking care not to be seen. It was easily possible with your porch to screen them. Naturally, the thought of someone entering your home troubled me even more.'

'All this was on your mind and you didn't tell me any of it?'

'Well, no. As Mr. Duffield says, there was no point in alarming you. I thought I'd dig a little deeper.'

Sipping his tea, Abbs studied Hetty, deciding she was coping well. They were a stoical family. She glanced at the mantel clock and her mouth tightened. He guessed she was thinking about her cat, as he continued.

'Someone could have entered this house through the rear garden gate. People don't lock their doors until dark but it would have to be someone who knew the house was empty. I started wondering who would want to frighten Miss Stephens. You're involved with the people who work in the shop. They would know when you were both out, for they'd see you go by.'

'Why should it be any of them? Did you think the errand boy would play such a cruel trick?'

Abbs hesitated, Hetty might not be a good judge of character but she was no fool. She'd pounced on the weak spot in his explanation. He'd given his word to Jane. He couldn't reveal he'd suspected her.

'I discounted the lad. For a while, I considered Arthur. I found the connecting door in the hall had been unbolted. That had to have been done by someone with access to this house. I thought that was how the parcel was left.'

'Arthur?' Hetty looked aghast. 'That's why you asked me about the door. Your profession's made you too cynical, Josiah. There's no bad in Arthur. He would never plot to frighten anyone.'

'I can see that now. You may be right about my work but after today, can you wonder if I take a jaundiced view at times?'

'I know I'll never be so trusting again.'

Duffield shifted on his hard chair. 'If I might say, ma'am, then that would be your boarder's worst damage.'

He seemed embarrassed as Hetty looked at him in surprise. 'Begging your pardon, Mrs Byers but you've made a lot of friends here. Most folk are decent and that's saying so with my job. Mr. Abbs probably sees it differently in a big town.'

'You're right, of course.' Hetty shivered. 'Forgive me, I'm not myself this evening, Mr. Duffield.'

'You're chilled, ma'am. All right if I put some more coal on for you?'

At her nod, Duffield arranged more knobs with great precision, tucking kindling between and taking a spill to set them ablaze. 'That should do it.' Producing a large spotted handkerchief, he dusted his fingers.

'I met Arthur when I was out walking on my first day here. He all but hinted he was thinking of making Miss Stephens an offer. He practically warned me off.'

'Good Lord, really? I'm starting to wonder if I know anybody. It was noticeable on Christmas Day that Arthur was attentive to Dora but it had gone that far?' Hetty shook her head wearily.

'I had the impression he's been keen on Miss Stephens since he first saw her but he wasn't getting anywhere. It's an old trick to frighten a woman, in order to be the one to comfort her. After all, he's almost part of the household and he's been longing to play her chivalrous protector.'

'He's had a fortunate escape,' said Hetty slowly. 'Only a couple of days ago, I was so pleased to see Dora happy with him.'

'She'd certainly switched her attention to him,' agreed Abbs drily. 'Though I believe Robert Fuller was the one she really wanted. Anyway, I decided I'd done Arthur an injustice. He isn't that devious.'

'So who did send the pig's head?'

'Why no one. Miss Stephens saw to the whole thing herself.'

Hetty's cup chinked in its saucer. 'But why? Was she mad? It would explain what she's done to my home.'

'I can't say. But she wouldn't be the first to stage a threat against herself. It's a ploy to get attention, everyone looking after her.' He'd put good money on Miss Stephens knowing of Jane's feelings for Fuller and trying to implicate her. 'She played the helpless victim of jealousy, so grateful for everyone's solicitude, I suppose?'

Hetty looked at Duffield. 'We were all very concerned.'

'She gave me the run around. Police hours wasted on trying to find the culprit. She was a good actress, dabbing at her eyes, real tears they were.'

'Amazing how many women can cry to order,' said Abbs dismissively. 'Or they use a smear of ointment just below the eyes. Not smelling-salts, the odour lingers. Can you think back to that day, Hetty? When you left, did she go back for something?'

'It was a while ago but now you've said it, I'm almost sure she did.' Hetty bit her lip as she thought. 'Why, Dora said she'd forgotten a letter she wanted to post and slipped back in the hall to get it. I think I waited on the pavement. That's when I noticed my neighbour working. I wouldn't have remembered, had you not pressed me. It was an ordinary day until we came home.'

'Would you have gone to your hall cupboard that day?'

She shook her head. 'I've been meaning to turn it out for a long time. Charley's fishing rod and net are still in there, Arthur didn't want them. No, I don't use it. You've seen we hang our things on the stand.'

'Then I've no doubt Miss Stephens concealed the box in there.' Abbs looked at Duffield. 'Will you repeat what you told me on the way here?'

'Gladly. Mr. Abbs asked me to make fresh enquiry of the butcher's in Reddenham, ma'am. To see if anyone recalled a woman, answering Miss Stephens's description, purchasing a pig's head that week. Bearing in mind, she couldn't have kept it for long. No one remembered her. Today, it came to me to enquire about the box instead. You showed it to me at the time and I had a description in my notebook.'

'That I do remember. It had a candy stripe.'

'So it did, ma'am. I've been back to Reddenham today. This time I asked at the haberdasher's.' Duffield paused for emphasis, 'and there our luck changed. The assistant remembered her all right. She'd been in several times buying packets of pins and threads. They were for you, I dare say.'

Hetty nodded. 'I get most things myself in Lynn but I've asked her to pick up some trifle while she was there.'

'She bought an identical box in the same week as the one found on your doorstep. Said it was for a present. The assistant was interested to know what it was but she didn't say. The woman remembered because she showed her a shallow box but Miss Stephens chose a deep, square one. There's no doubt whatsoever. She faked the whole thing.'

She looks like she's aged ten years, thought Abbs. He hadn't felt the need to see Hetty often because she would always be there in Norfolk, far at the back of his mind. An intimation of her mortality touched him with a cold finger-tip.

'I'm glad she's gone,' Hetty said finally. 'It's so deceitful. Only a warped mind could think of that. Why did she unbolt the hall door, do you think?'

'To deflect suspicion on to Arthur, Grace or Jane,' said Abbs. 'I kept asking questions. I think she saw me checking it on Christmas Eve, early in the morning. Later that day, when your neighbours were here, someone was listening behind the back door when Constable Duffield and I were speaking outside.'

'She did ask me all about you. I said you were a very good detective.' Hetty tried her tea and felt the pot. 'So she did all this damage in a fit of pique and ran away because she guessed you'd worked out her secret? I'm not surprised she felt too ashamed to face us.'

He didn't want to continue this. 'No, Hetty. I'm afraid there's something worse.'

'Perhaps we should leave it for tonight,' said Duffield.

'I'll make some fresh tea. I don't want to be treated like a child, just because I'm a woman. I'd rather get it all over with now, than face more in the morning.' Refusing their offers of help, Hetty left the room.

Abbs sighed, leaning back and staring at the ceiling. His head was beginning to throb. Their hours in Hunstanton felt like months ago. So much for the curative properties of sea air.

The ticking of the clock irritated him, then the long-case one in the hall chimed the hour with a deeper note. Moving to the window, he wrenched at the curtain.

'You were right. It's starting to snow.'

Duffield joined him. He moved easily for a big man. They stood watching the first flakes drifting silently to the ground. The moonlight was insufficient to show whether they vanished on impact with the earth and tiles. Time would tell.

'What a mess.'

'I see it like lancing a boil,' said Duffield.

'What?' Abbs grunted at him, too exhausted to be polite. In the course of a few days, it seemed he and Ezra Duffield had ventured beyond professional acquaintance.

'It's all blood and pus. So foul, you wish you'd left well alone. Hurts like buggery but it's better done. Like straightening Jane out. Painful for her but necessary. Don't leave things festering. Isn't that what the Stephens woman did?'

'You're quite a philosopher. So the wound will be sore for a time but heal cleanly?'

'Better out than in. You wouldn't be making fun of me, Mr. Abbs? It does sound quaint out loud.'

'Far from it. I was wondering why you weren't promoted, long ago?'

'I do believe I got in the sergeant's way when I worked out of Lynn. Kept treading on his toes.' Duffield grinned at him.

Abbs knew it was the only answer he was going to get. They stood in a friendly silence, as inch by inch, Aylmer was steadily whitened.

The door knob rattled clumsily, though Abbs had caught no clink of china being carried. Hetty appeared, her arms full of a large cat who was submitting on sufferance but wriggling. Possibly with supper on his mind.

'Look who I've found. I heard a familiar thud and ran to the door. It's where Smut comes over the wash-house roof. He seems his usual self. Did you know it's started to snow?' Relief was shining across her tired face as she bent her head against his fur.

'I'm so glad, Hetty.'

'We've often passed the time of day when I've been digging out the back.' Duffield approached diffidently and rubbed behind Smut's ears.

'I hope he doesn't do any damage among your vegetables?'

'I like moggies, ma'am. He's more than welcome to see off the pigeons.'

'Do you think he's been frightened? I do wonder what he saw.'

'He doesn't look scared,' said Abbs. 'Just feed the beast.'

'There's some melts for him in the larder, I'll be back directly.' Hetty smiled broadly at them both. 'I don't give a fig for what Mrs Merrick has to say about her costume. Nothing matters now Smut's safe.'

She allowed Constable Duffield to follow her to the scullery. With the door left open, Abbs could hear snatches of their conversation. Hetty thanked him for the flowers, enquiring how he'd managed to save them from frost. Duffield explained something about glass jars and straw.

He rather thought a start had been made, fragile as the pale hellebores, and as easily crushed.

'What else d'you have to tell me, Josiah?'

This time Duffield had carried in the tray and Hetty's hands lay folded in her lap. Her face was composed as she regarded him.

He'd been glad of the small respite. 'There's no gentle way to say this, Hetty. I believe Dora Stephens caused Bob Fuller's death.'

Whatever she had been expecting, it was not that. 'That's ridiculous.. I'm sorry, Josiah, I shouldn't have put it like that but surely you aren't saying Dora pushed him in front of a train? That's cold-blooded murder. It isn't as if he died on the platform, how could she have done it? Besides, she was here all afternoon.'

'I don't think she pushed him,' said Abbs patiently. 'And I didn't say murder. Nor do I believe what took place was cold-blooded.'

'I don't understand.' Hetty turned to Duffield, who remained silent, giving her a sympathetic look.

'I'm about to explain. You said that on the afternoon Bob Fuller died, Miss Stephens had felt unwell and gone up to lie down. Did you look in on her, or could she have left the house without your knowing?'

'I didn't disturb her because I wasn't there. I called round to see my friend Mrs Hunt. You met her here on Christmas Eve. It was coming up to her daughter's birthday and I'd made a pinny for her.'

'Did Miss Stephens know you were going out?'

'Certainly. When two women share a house they know everything about one another's doings. At least, I thought I did. She insisted she was best off trying to sleep.'

'Where does Mrs Hunt live?'

'Along the main street. Why?'

'If Miss Stephens went out the back way, taking the path through the trees, you wouldn't have bumped into her. Was she in her room when you returned?'

Shaking her head, Hetty kept her gaze fixed on Abbs. 'In the garden. I remember that day well because of hearing about Bob the next morning. It was nearly dark when I got back. I went straight outside to fill the coal scuttle and found Dora. She said she'd come down for some air. She really did look poorly and she couldn't manage any supper that night.'

Raising his eyebrows at Duffield, Abbs felt a quiet satisfaction. So much for Miss Stephens's alibi. Hetty had both provided and demolished it.

'I think Miss Stephens slipped out of the house and went to waylay Bob Fuller, as he came home from visiting Mrs Tillson.'

'Until today I'd have said the idea was insane. But now I don't know what she was capable of.'

'Would she have been likely to know he was visiting Mrs Tillson that day?'

Hetty wrinkled her brow as she thought. 'Arthur keeps Grace and Jane back once a month for stock-taking. Bob knew Grace would be late home that day. Maggie Tillson would be on her own for longer.' She made an impatient gesture with her hand, 'I don't know any more, Josiah.'

'I believe Dora Stephens wanted to marry Bob Fuller. Whether she was desperate for a home or she cared for him, I can't say. Perhaps both, though the facts point to the latter. After all, if she wanted to catch any suitable husband, she'd successfully reeled in Arthur.'

'When Bob first came, I thought he and Dora were going to make a match. She was pretty, gentle and kind in her ways, a good housekeeper. She seemed ideal for him and they were walking out together.' Hetty looked almost pleadingly at him. 'Did I get everything so wrong? Didn't you see them together, Mr. Duffield?'

'I can't really say I did, ma'am. As far as I could tell, Bob was friendly to everyone alike. Gossip was that they were courting at first but I didn't see it for myself.'

'She had a good home with me.'

'No one could be kinder,' said Abbs. 'But women want to be mistress of their own home, don't they? People have killed before now to be secure. It's a rare woman who doesn't want to marry and have children.' Cursing inwardly, he continued swiftly without catching Hetty's eye. 'It's a precarious life for any woman without a man, unless she has financial independence.'

'That's true enough. I told you Dora was sewing for her bottom drawer.'

'So you did. I don't know why she chose that particular day. Perhaps Mr. Fuller had said something that made her feel her chance was slipping away. Remember what Mrs Tillson told us. He'd settled his arrangements with his betrothed. If Miss Stephens wanted to get him on his own and talk to him without being observed, what better place than the short-cut through the wood? She could hardly call on him. The only place she could see him was in his shop, where anyone could interrupt them.'

Hetty nodded, acknowledging the truth of his remarks. 'What made you think all this in the first place? Was it your profession?'

He could tell she wanted to put off what he was about to relate. 'I suppose so. You get an instinct for something being wrong. When you described your neighbour's death, it sounded curious. People take a good deal of care when they use a railway crossing. Presumably he'd been here long enough to know when the trains are passing. When I saw the spot, I found a clear view in both directions, even at dusk. Trains are heard long before they're in sight. I wondered if he was intoxicated. It might even have been self-murder.'

Hetty pressed her hand to her mouth. 'Not Bob, he took such pleasure in the small things of life. He was pleased to see the martins building in his eaves last summer. The only time I ever saw him cross was soon after he came. When Arthur wanted to knock the nests down with a pole.'

'Did he, indeed?'

Hetty made an apologetic face. 'They made a great mess on the pavement. Bob said they were his eaves. He wouldn't let Arthur do it.'

'Quite right,' said Duffield.

She gave him a rueful smile. 'Arthur didn't mean to be harsh, he didn't think. He will have everything orderly.'

'Mrs Tillson told us when Mr. Fuller left her cottage,' said Abbs. 'At least five and twenty minutes before the train was due. She couldn't understand why he was knocked down. He had to have been intercepted and something happen. Or why was he on the crossing, unable to save himself?'

The one-sided throbbing was echoing through his head, like the pistons of a railway engine. Abbs imagined the relentless nearing of the great iron beast. The chugging building in intensity, red sparks flying in the dusk. Did damp clouds of coughing steam envelop Fuller, hiding the monster until the roaring onslaught burst through? How much awareness of terror did he have, before the buffers pushed him into merciful oblivion?

Shuddering, Abbs attempted to clear his thoughts. 'Everyone told me something different about Miss Stephens and Bob Fuller. You assumed they were courting because you thought they were well suited. And you want everyone to be happy. Arthur said she wasn't interested in Fuller and accepted an invitation or two, merely out of politeness. He was jealous. You both saw what you wanted to see. Jane Goddard thought Miss Stephens meant to win Fuller. She had a different impression.'

Hetty looked at him in surprise. 'Have you been interviewing everyone in the village?'

'No, don't worry. No one knows anything of this outside this room. Finally, Mrs Tillson told me the truth as Bob Fuller saw it. She had it from the man himself. Remember how angry you were on Miss Stephens's behalf?'

'I was stunned to hear he was betrothed all the time we knew him.'

'How would Dora Stephens feel if Fuller told her his affections were given elsewhere? That he'd soon be bringing his new wife to live two doors away. The new Mrs Fuller would be the centre of attention in the village. People would gossip about Miss Stephens having lost her chance. Wouldn't she feel humiliated?'

Duffield leant forward. 'I know it's a lot to take in, Mrs Byers, but what I saw in your sewing-room shocked me, I don't mind admitting. That was the work of an ungovernable temper.'

Hetty nodded unhappily. 'When I saw my scissors poking out of the bodice.. I think Dora must be insane. But she hid it so well.'

'We can only surmise what passed between them,' said Abbs, his voice grim. 'Fuller must have made it clear he had no interest in her. I think she saw red and attacked him. As Mr. Duffield says, the proof's here in what she did this morning. Most likely he'd turned away from her. She picked up a branch – there are plenty lying around there - and struck him. Either on the head or possibly, he slipped and hit his head in falling.'

He paused, watching to see she wasn't about to collapse. Hetty was as white and still as the holly he could just glimpse outside, where he'd left the curtains carelessly parted.

'Did she mean to kill him, do you think?' Hetty's lips were stiff, her voice low.

'We'll never know. In a single moment of rage, perhaps. Whatever happened, I imagine she fled. Self-preservation takes over in most people. I doubt she killed Mr. Fuller. What I think happened is something like this. She lashes out at him and races back here, fleeing from the consequences of what she's done. She hurries through the back gate just in time and is still in the garden when you appear. So she pretends to have come downstairs for some fresh air.' Abbs looked at Duffield. 'Does that sound feasible?'

Duffield nodded, his features impassive. 'It does.'

'Meanwhile Fuller is knocked down, possibly stunned. He gets up, I can't know how badly he was injured, but I'm guessing he was dazed. His one thought is to get aid. He stumbles back in the direction he came from, making for Mrs Tillson's cottage across the railway track.'

In view of Hetty's sensibilities, he left it there. She looked out at the snow. He wasn't sure she saw the scene outside or had taken in what he said. There was a moment of silence, save for the crackle of the fire. Then Duffield's boots creaked as he shifted.

'If a hint of this had come up at the time, there'd have been evidence. She might have broken down under questioning and we'd have looked for the branch. There'd have been bl...' Catching Abbs's quick movement, he remembered where he was and subsided. 'Begging your pardon, Mrs Byers. I was thinking professionally.'

Hetty murmured something.

'What did you say?' Abbs spoke sharply as he leant towards her.

Her eyes met his. 'I said, *Not a branch*. It wasn't a branch she hit him with,' her voice trailed away.

'Tell me what you mean, Hetty. Take your time.'

'Dora's cane went missing. I didn't notice for a few days until we went out. When I asked her, she said she must have left it on the train. She'd gone to Lynn the day after we heard about Bob's death. But she didn't mention her loss when she came home.'

'Did she enquire at the lost luggage office?' said Duffield.

'I suggested that but she wouldn't. She said there was no point in going all the way back to town. Someone was sure to have taken it. I couldn't understand why she wouldn't try.'

'I mind seeing her with it,' said Duffield. 'An expensive one if I'm not mistaken.'

'It was a dressmaker's cane. The kind where the handle unscrews and there's a tiny compartment inside with a thimble, needle and thread for emergency repairs.'

Duffield leapt to his feet, his fist clenched. 'That's it, Mr. Abbs, we've got her. Surely we can do something now?'

'Yes, I believe we can,' said Abbs slowly. 'It's still conjecture but we have a weight of circumstantial evidence. If we could find her and get a confession..' He came to a decision. 'I think I'd better travel to Lynn myself in the morning. We'll both go and lay this before your inspector.'

'How can the police find her, Josiah?'

'A lot will depend on chance but it's our duty to try. We can get her papered at least, a description circulated in The *Police Gazette* and trace something of where she went.'

'Not Manchester, at any rate,' said Duffield.

'Will I have to give evidence in court?'

'If she's taken up, yes. You would do it?'

Silence again. Abbs exchanged glances with Duffield. They both knew what Hetty was thinking.

'Will she hang if you catch her?'

His voice was even, as if he was remarking on the weather. 'I shouldn't think so. The charge would be manslaughter at worst, or assault if she was lucky. Everything would depend on whether she confessed. She could plead provocation, you see and no one could prove otherwise. Chances are, she'd get off. But Constable Duffield's right, we must try.'

His features hardened as he pictured Dora Stephens in the dock, all submissive and lady-like. Facing the rows of male jurors with her tremulous voice and a handkerchief to her eye. He didn't add that if convicted of manslaughter, she would serve a stiff gaol sentence.

A man was dead and in his opinion she deserved it.

~

'I wish you'd let me make you some sandwiches.'

He should have agreed. Too late, Abbs realised he'd deprived Hetty of an affectionate gesture and a need to be occupied.

'Your excellent breakfast will keep me going for the whole journey.'

Now the time for parting was near, there was more constraint between them than when they'd met. The trap had not been offered or requested. The two of them had walked to the station.

He'd been touched when Jane and Grace had called in after work on the previous evening to bid him farewell.

'Can I ask you something, Josiah?'

'Of course.'

'What would you have done if Dora hadn't fled?'

'I truly don't know, Hetty. All I do know is I'd have done something. I would not have gone away, leaving you with her.'

He was profoundly relieved matters had come to a head. If Dora Stephens hadn't eavesdropped on his conversation with Duffield on Christmas Eve, she wouldn't have known he was looking into Fuller's death. If Grace hadn't suggested meeting her mother, or Mrs Tillson hadn't told him that Fuller left long before the train was due, he would never have had the ammunition which broke her nerve.

Patting his arm, Hetty left his side and moved to the open door. The sound of a spade scraping could be heard outside. 'Thomas is hard at work clearing the snow.'

The station-master had been performing the same task the previous morning, when he and Ezra Duffield had taken the train to King's Lynn. A long, explanatory interview with the inspector in charge had ensued. Finally they'd left, knowing they'd done everything possible to set the forces of law and order in motion.

The events of the past week had forged a firm understanding between them. By the time they returned wearily to Aylmer, Abbs knew that Duffield would be a staunch friend to Hetty. He felt sure they would meet again some day.

'What will you do now, Hetty?'

'Me? Oh, I shall do very well. You mustn't worry about me. I'll work by day, visit my friends and in the evenings I'll sit by the fire and read, with Smut on my lap.' She smiled brightly at him and he knew there was no more to be said.

'What about your business?'

'I shall tell Mrs Merrick that Miss Stephens left after accidentally spilling ink over her commission. She can wait while I begin again or do as she pleases.'

'It occurred to me that as you don't want another boarder, you might think of taking on Jane as your assistant.'

'Jane? Do you think she'd be interested?'

'She's unhappy in the shop and you do know her. Whether she could manage the work, I couldn't say.'

'That isn't a problem. I've seen her plain work and I could soon teach her. It would be a great relief not to take on a stranger. Thank you, Josiah. I'll invite her to tea.'

'No need to mention it wasn't your idea.' Abbs glanced at the waiting-room clock. 'We'd better go outside, I think.'

Ushering her ahead, he picked up his travelling case. No one else was waiting for the London train. As they stood on the wet, newly exposed platform, a mound of snow dislodged from the canopy, landing with a soft thud on the track.

'Thank heavens the trains are running. I know it's important you get back, though I'm sorry to see you go. You've had an awful time here and I meant it to be such a happy Christmas.'

'You mustn't get upset. Remember what we said last night? We'll both look to the future.'

'I shall. I'm sorry Arthur didn't come to see you off. He's terribly upset and feels he's been kept in the dark but he'll come round.'

'His pride's been hurt and he's out of pocket. He'll live.'

Explaining everything slowly to Arthur had been far more difficult than speaking to a fellow detective. The three of them agreed that Arthur had to know, but not the rest of the village.

Time enough if Miss Stephens was ever found and, provided she never came to the attention of the police, that seemed unlikely. If she was ever taken up for any offence, her past would catch up with her.

Though in Abbs's opinion, wherever she took herself next, it would be under a different name.

The signalman was moving about in his box and the London train was due. It was not lost on Abbs that Miss Stephens had caught this train only two days earlier. How ill at ease she must have been, desperate to get away. All the while, putting on a front to fool Arthur.

Had she been still seething with anger as a result of his own actions?

'I hate goodbyes,' said Hetty.

The signal jerked into position, a distant, rhythmic chugging filled the quiet morning. The train had just gone over the crossing-place. Abbs tried not to think about Bob Fuller.

'Then don't say them. I'll try and write more often. And you must come and see me next time, have a change from Aylmer.'

A jaunty, echoing hoot and the engine came in sight, wreathed in smoke.

'I'd love to visit you. You're a fine detective, Jo. Don't let that superintendent of yours tell you any different.'

Abbs, laughing at Hetty's fierce expression, kissed her and grasped his case.

Once aboard, he waited at the window of his compartment door. Hetty was saying something else as she smiled and held her handkerchief.

'What's that?'

'I said where will I come and visit you? Do you know?'

His reply was drowned by Thomas blowing his whistle. The words dispelled in the steam as they stood waving. The locomotive juddered and moved off.

When the station was gone, Abbs sank down in a corner of the empty compartment, his hat at his side.

He rather hoped it would be London.

The End

Now try our 1930s detective novel *The Seafront Corpse,* featuring Inspector Eddie Chance...

Sussex 1931

There were always ways to make money if you had the nous.

Despite the Depression, he had nothing but contempt for those who didn't. The newspaper he'd found on the train had been full of the usual whining from disgruntled miners. All it took was a visit from the Prince of Wales and they'd trot off happily to the Labour Exchange, thinking someone cared. What fools people were.

He'd passed on the station buffet for the best tea-room Tennysham had on offer. Upstairs in Grove's department store, it had still been Grove's Drapery Bazaar when he'd first known it. The ground floor stank of good perfume and greasy cosmetics. Blank-faced assistants faking an interest in old women in furs. One was rubbing cream on the back of a brown blotched hand, veins heavier than the rings. She caught his eye and smiled, the mask real for an instant. He winked.

The tea-room was fairly full at that time of the afternoon and Leslie Warrender took a seat in the window where two rigidly corseted matrons had just left. The table was still to be cleared. He moved a saucer and pocketed the threepenny bit underneath as he consulted the menu. The waitress came up to him, looking flustered.

'I'm really sorry, sir, I'll straighten this for you. We're short-staffed today and the lunch-time rush isn't long over.'

'That's quite all right. Not too early for afternoon tea, am I?'

She hesitated, glancing at the large rectangular clock. He bestowed a boyish smile that made her forget her aching feet.

'Oh no, not at all, sir. We've just started. Are you ready to order?'

'I rather think I'll try the set tea.'

'Very good, sir.'

He tucked into his food as soon as it came. Looked down at the passers-by, blurred beneath the long glass verandah. Across the street he watched a blind man standing patiently with a tray of

93

shoe-laces. His head turned, following the sound of footsteps going past. Sorry chum, the world's moved on. Nobody wanted to see the maimed haunting street corners, reminding them.

It amused him to think how well-heeled he must look when all he had was a pound note in his pocket. When he'd finished eating, he took out a match-book and a finely tooled silver case. It was inscribed with initials that had happened to be his. Tapping an expensive Sullivan, he lit up and sat back, blowing smoke elegantly.

A third-rate pianist had started tinkling softly in the background and he watched the other customers from his vantage point by a fern on a wooden stand. You could learn a lot from watching people, especially women and he was out of practice. A shaft of bitterness fell like a shadow across the table.

Forget that. The past was over and done with. What mattered now was a bright future. What a provincial dump Tennysham was. A few months ago he'd never intended to see it again. Then fate had handed him an unexpected reminder. He wasn't one for looking back and his time working here seemed like a lifetime ago.

The waitress broke into his thoughts, tucking the bill by a plate and removing the cake stand. Her eager, shiny face left him cold. Decent legs though.

There'd been a girl in Tennysham who'd had good legs. No money to speak of but very pretty. She'd been eager. If women only knew how that brought out the worst in a man. He went for women who looked indifferent. Sleek hair, perfectly groomed, their perfume wafting money.

Carrying his small case, he walked out into the High Street. A weak sun was breaking through the clouds. In the window a sign suggested *Pastels For Spring* before a display of hats and light gloves draped across hand-bags.

A unwanted memory stirred of the downs in springtime. Nature walks from infant school, the mournful bleating of lambs and a feeling of freedom. High on the green ramparts overlooking the Channel, as the Romans had when they marched along the dirty cream tracks.

He'd lie in bed, reading about the smugglers who used those ways by night. No hidden coves in Sussex. Long pebble beaches and perilous paths, steeper than trench ladders up the chalk clefts. He'd fall asleep to the sound of boys' voices drifting from the chapel. Long before the war when the world was different.

Only a fool was sentimental about childhood. He'd had far too much time to think. Revisiting old stamping grounds never did anyone any good. He supposed it was because his old ma was dead. Women never stopped believing in him. Well, he was about to collect a fresh start. Who needed a pallid English spring when the parasols would be out on the Riviera?

The rows of streets behind the sea-front all looked the same. Starchy, scrubbed, wearing their facades like uniforms. Down at heel but fighting a rear-guard action. The ugly bulk of a gas-works rose above the chimney pots and gulls circled like vultures.

Pearl-street, chosen at random had several houses with *Room To Let* propped in their bay window. On a whim he stopped at number nineteen, his birthday. Clean nets, a red geranium and *Aberfeldy* on the glass over the door.

The woman who answered his knock was holding a tea cloth. He flicked on the charm, as instant as electric lighting. Her other hand touched her inexpertly-styled hair. The sum she named was the going rate, he supposed. Her expression was sympathetic as she looked at his case.

'Salesman are you?'

'Insurance agent.' It was the first thing that came into his head. He believed in thinking on his feet. Say brushes or cloths and she might want to see some samples.

'Would you be wanting an evening meal?'

'Better not. I'd be coming and going. I've an old friend to look up while I'm in the area.'

'That's nice for you. It's the room at the front so there's a sea view of a sort.'

She smiled in a defeated kind of way as she held the door wider. Flattening herself against the wallpaper so he could climb the stairs first. A nice woman with hope in her eyes. She needed the money. Wedding ring worn thin, a widow, he'd bet.

'It's the first on the left.'

There was a brief moment when he wondered if the house was paid off. She couldn't be more than late forties. In another life she'd be pathetically grateful for someone like him to take an interest. He'd be doing her a favour, take her out of herself.

He had bigger fish to fry.

Four days later

'That man's still there.'

Ivy Betts paused in the window of number three, her arms full of clean bed-linen. Across the road sea and sky were merged in dull grey, the colour her dad called *feldgrau*. He was a bit of a card, her dad, throwing in the odd French word, which made her mum's lips tighten and singing snatches of French songs while he worked on his bike.

It looked as though it might rain. She watched as an elderly couple came in view with a small white dog. As they passed the sea-front shelter where the man sat in a corner, they slowed as though considering joining him. Ivy knew she should get on but couldn't resist watching the small tableau. They would exchange good mornings 'cause that was what you said. Then they'd laugh and have a word about the weather, *could be worse*, as they settled themselves.

Only it didn't happen. The dog started to turn in. The old couple stuck their heads in and thought better of it, the woman tugging at the dog's leash in a dumb show of disapproval.

'Come away, Ivy. The beds won't make themselves.'

'Yes, Miss Aldridge. Sorry.' She'd better look lively. Ivy began to flatten the bottom sheet over the mattress, averting her eyes from a small irregular stain on the ticking. Her dad would say it was the shape of Belgium.

Her employer watched her work. 'It's a wicked waste after two nights, the price the laundry charges.'

Ivy framed an understanding expression but made no comment as she moved to each corner.

'What was so interesting outside?'

'Only a man in the shelter over the way. He's been there a long time and he doesn't seem to move. I saw him on my way to work. I wondered if he's poorly or unhappy.'

Miss Aldridge sniffed. She had a language of them and she, Mrs Thompson and Eric, the boot boy all knew what each one meant.

'You shouldn't be wasting your time wondering about things that don't concern you.'

'A couple did look in the shelter. I suppose he can't be ill.'

'There you are then.' Taking up her pince-nez, she focused on the scene across the esplanade. The cord dangled against her flat chest. 'Hmm, looks respectable enough from the back. He's probably asleep. Now, Ivy, don't you forget to save the soap this time. There's plenty of girls would be glad of your position, you know.'

'Yes, Miss, I won't.'

She didn't risk pulling a face behind her back. Her employer had eyes in the back of her head and she needed this job. Finishing the bed, Ivy wiped a row of stubble from the basin before reaching for the drum of Dawn and shaking out a meagre amount. The remaining sliver of soap held a curly dark hair like a question mark.

She'd got in terrible trouble last week when she'd thrown away the tiny heel of a bar, which Miss Aldridge had retrieved from the kitchen bin. They were to be softened, coaxed together and worked into a new bar for one of the cheaper rooms.

The Belvedere wasn't one of the best hotels along the sea-front, whatever Miss Aldridge thought. Situated at the less favoured end of town where the buildings started to peter out, you had a fair walk to the pier and the rooms at the back overlooked the roof-top of the bus depot.

It was a commercial-hotel with a few winter residents. They catered for holidaying families though it was too early in the year for those. The beach did have a stretch of sand between the grey pebbles but that was down the other end too.

It occurred to her that Miss Aldridge was more hard up than she let on. When she first came, her employer had always worn a large sapphire ring. Ugly with an old-fashioned claw setting, she'd once mentioned it had belonged to her mother. Come to think of it, she hadn't noticed it for a while.

What's more, Miss Aldridge hadn't found a replacement for Meg which meant twice as much work fell on her shoulders. And only that morning Mrs Thompson complained the meat order had to be cheaper every week.

Her dad always said she thought too much. *No sense worrying over strangers, girl. They wouldn't do the same for you.* Bundling the used linen into the basket on the landing, Ivy decided she'd think about something cheerful while she did the brass. Rushed off her feet serving the breakfasts, she'd earned a sit-down.

The Seafront Corpse

Set in 1931, newly promoted Inspector Eddie Chance is  back in his home town. Reunited with his old pal Sergeant Bishop in the sleepy Sussex town of Tennysham-on-Sea. The only cloud on their horizon is a young police-woman with ambitions to be a detective.

The seaside resort is getting ready for the first day trippers of the season. When the body of a stranger is found on the promenade, Inspector Chance is faced with a baffling murder...

A traditional 1930s murder mystery set in a vanished England of typewriters, telephone boxes and tweeds.

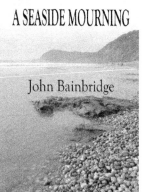

A SEASIDE MOURNING

John Bainbridge

A SEASIDE MOURNING - An atmospheric Victorian murder mystery. Devonshire 1873. In the sleepy seaside resort of Seaborough, a leading resident may have been poisoned, Still coming to terms with his own mourning, Inspector Abbs is sent to uncover the truth. Behind the Nottingham lace curtains, certain residents have their secrets. Under growing pressure, Abbs and Sergeant Reeve must search the past for answers as they try to unmask a killer.

Connect with us at:

Our writing blog: www.johnbainbridgewriter.wordpress.com

and on Twitter at:

@stravaigerjohn

Follow us on Goodreads:

https://www.goodreads.com/author/show/73470,John_Bainbridge

Printed in Great Britain
by Amazon

40623587R00061